MW01359284

Michelle Gallant

Feels Like Home

While this is a work of fiction, it draws on elements of real-life experiences. To protect the privacy of individuals and respect personal boundaries, names, identifying details, and certain events have been changed or reimagined. Any resemblance to actual people, places, or events is purely coincidental.

Author photo by Amanda Rentiers Photography

Cover image inspired by an original photograph taken by Carly Gallant, used with permission. Digitally altered and adapted using AI tools.

Amazon Paperback ISBN: 9798346608424
Amazon Hardcover ISBN: 9798286774562

Printed and bound in Canada

To connect with Michelle:
Instagram: @mgallantcreative
Email: michellegallantbooks@gmail.com

A NOTE FROM THE AUTHOR

While this story is a work of fiction, it's woven with threads of real-life experience—some of which may be difficult to read. Themes of divorce, emotional abuse, and mental health appear throughout the book. I understand these subjects can feel heavy or triggering. If you're not in a place to face those moments right now, it's okay to pause, skip ahead, or come back when you're ready.

This story isn't just about the hard parts. It's also about healing, resilience, and the power of choosing yourself.

Through these pages, I hope you find not only reflection but also reassurance—that growth can come from the most unexpected places. The goal isn't to feel regret, guilt, or shame for the choices you've made. There are no "wrong" decisions—only the ones that were right for you at the time. Use them as lessons. Let them be the opportunities that help you grow.

Be clear with what you want.

And watch as your whole life flips upside down to make it happen.

Trust Yourself.

And when you can't trust yourself, *trust your dog.*

PROLOGUE

This is a story about staying too long, about pouring yourself into places that were never meant to hold you. About waking up one day and realizing the life you built doesn't feel like yours anymore.

If you've ever second-guessed your worth, shrunk yourself to be loved, or stayed for the potential…this is for you.

You don't have to beg for what's meant for you.
You won't need to chase it or convince it to choose you.
When it's right, it'll feel like peace. Like an exhale. Like a hot cup of coffee and a good book on a quiet morning.

But first, you'll have to burn the version of your life you thought you wanted.
And yeah… it's going to hurt…

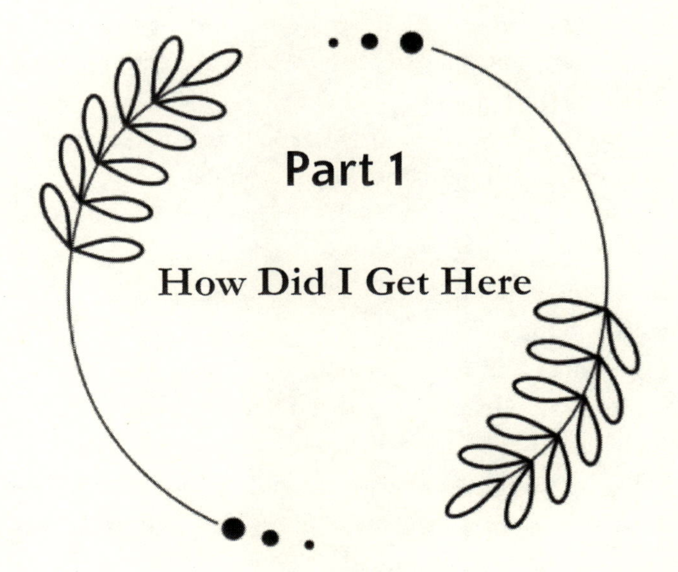

Part 1

How Did I Get Here

Chapter 1

Instagram is a dangerous place at one-thirty in the morning. I scrolled past curated lives, vacations, engagements, baby announcements, and bodies that looked too perfect to be real. I knew better than to compare. Still, the posts seeped in, one after another: smiling couples gushing about their "soulmates," and swearing they "couldn't live without each other." It made me want to vomit. So cringey.

We all knew the truth.

Those couples probably sat at opposite ends of the couch, barely speaking, scrolling through their phones. She hid her online shopping. He hid his second Instagram account full of bikini likes.

I should have been asleep. Instead, I was wired. Maybe it was the coffee I had at eight o'clock. Maybe it was just the sleeplessness that had haunted me for months. I was tired though. Tired of chasing the next thing. Tired of always being "on." Tired of pretending I wanted to go out every night. Tired of pretending I had it all together.

I lay in my queen-sized bed, the first one I hadn't shared with another human for over 12 years. Mischa, my 12-year-old Husky, was curled up beside me, loyal as ever. Not too close, not too far. Mischa had been with me through everything: every move, the sad moments, the adventures. She officially became mine when she was four, though she felt like mine long before that. Even with her beside me, the bed felt massive. Empty in a way that wasn't about size.

The silence of my new apartment wrapped around me as I scrolled mindlessly, desperate for distraction. I spent the last six months trying to fill the hollowness that came after separating from my husband, Josh.

From the outside, my life looked perfect.

- Big, beautiful wedding.
- The house.
- The "perfect" dog.
- A thriving book review business.
- Solo travel.
- Smiling selfies.
- Curated captions: *I don't know where I'd be without you. Love of my life.*

Looking back at those posts now made my skin crawl. Not because I was bitter, but because I had edited my own reality. I had been so desperate to believe it was true, I sold a version of my life that I couldn't live in.

The apartment was part of a triplex. The shared parking lot was always busy with tenants coming and going. I wasn't thrilled about living in a basement unit but it was what I could afford in a decent part of the city. It was bigger than I expected, almost nine hundred square feet, just enough space to start over. The walls were mostly bare. I hadn't decided yet which memories deserved to be hung. Earlier, I had burned a cinnamon candle to make the space feel less foreign; its faint sweetness still lingered in the air.

The kitchen floors were cold linoleum, flowing into the small living room. A medium-sized area rug, snagged for cheap on Facebook Marketplace, added the only softness. Its outdated appliances whirred and hummed with every use.

In the bedroom, a thrifted bedside lamp bathed the walls in soft, golden light. This room was my sanctuary. My retreat. The place where Mischa always waited for me. When I first moved in, I splurged on a new bedding set, one I couldn't really afford and was still paying off. Feminine, cloud-soft, a small luxury I refused to apologize for.

The living room, with its secondhand couch and TV — good enough to re-watch the entire Sex and The City series.

But here, in this room, I could finally breathe. I packed my clothes. All of my books. The spare bed. And Mischa. She was the only thing I couldn't walk away from. If Josh had kept her, I'd be lost—more lost than I already was.

I sold the rest of the brand-name clothes, purses, shoes, things I'd bought with money I didn't have to convince the world I was thriving. I was barely surviving.

Now, looking at it all from a distance, I couldn't believe how little any of it mattered. The life I had worked so hard to curate didn't fit anymore. It wasn't who I wanted to be. It never really was.

I always thought I wanted to get married. That's what you do, right? You fall in love, throw the big wedding, buy the house, have kids, and live happily ever after. For years, I nagged Josh about getting married. I was so eager to plan the wedding that I didn't really think about what marriage meant. I got lost in the details: table décor, seating charts, wedding party lists and ignored what should have been the foundation of our future. But the truth? I didn't know how to be in an adult relationship.

I had grown up watching my parents, and well, I wouldn't exactly call that a perfect or loving relationship. They fought constantly. Josh and I didn't fight at all, not really. Instead, we held everything in until it all exploded. We were both just doing the best we could with what we had.

I invested so much time, energy, and money into planning the wedding, obsessing over flowers, dresses, and whether to invite that girl from high school I barely remembered. But I didn't spend any time thinking about what it takes to build a strong, lasting marriage. I look back on that wedding day now and wonder how everyone saw it. Perfect. Gorgeous even. And it was. It was beautiful. But all I remember is dancing once. I skipped the dinner I'd carefully curated so I could make sure everyone else was having a good time. Josh and I barely had a chance to be present with each other. By 2 a.m., we collapsed into bed like we'd just run a marathon. Not exactly the romantic ending I had dreamed of. It definitely wasn't how I thought it would be.

Josh and I were together for 12 years, married for two of them. We'd been so young when we got together. I was 18. And while he wasn't my first, he was my first love. I had only been with one other person before him.

We don't get married expecting to get divorced. We don't get into relationships with the idea that they'll end. For a long time, I told myself this was forever. I mean, isn't that what marriage is supposed to be? But there's something they don't tell you, forever isn't a given. Nothing is forever. Forever only works if it's a journey both people want to stay on. It takes work, effort, and a mutual willingness to grow together. In our case, I didn't need more of the same. I needed something different. But I didn't know how to ask for it.

Just because two people decide to be together doesn't mean the passion, effort, and communication should fade away. At the start of a relationship, you do things to win each other. But those things shouldn't stop just because you've already won each other. I didn't know how to move past that.

I needed to figure out who I was, without him, without anyone. This was the first time I was truly alone. There was work to do. A lot of it. Codependency. Childhood trauma. Communication issues. Rage I hadn't fully acknowledged. Feelings I didn't even have words for. I felt guilty, like I was betraying him by simply feeling… lost. And when I tried to tell him, my words just bounced off, unheard.

Near the end, I'd sit in my car in the driveway, dreading going inside. Some nights, it felt easier to sleep on the lawn than walk through that front door. (Figuratively, not literally.) I kept asking myself, is this it? There was this nagging belief that I was meant for a life full of more, more spontaneity, more discovery, more change. Josh, though? He loved predictability. He liked knowing exactly what the next day would look like, and making just enough to get by. I didn't want to just get by. I wanted to travel, to support each other's growth, to go to events together. But all I did was go alone. So, I buried myself in work and travelled when I could, alone.

I didn't want to be at home. I wanted to be living my life, gathering experiences.

He would have given me the moon if I had asked, but because of my avoidance, lack of communication, and plain ignorance, I walked away. We were growing apart, but I wasn't capable or willing to address the deep-rooted issue: I didn't know how to communicate in a way that could be heard. I didn't have the tools to express my feelings so he could understand. And he didn't think we had any issues, until I let them all out one night. I had my faults. He did too. It took him far too long to look at himself, like, really look at himself and see if he even liked who was looking back. On top of that, I had no prior relationship experience to fall back on. Everything was so surface-level and I needed to go deeper..

My thoughts often circled back to one of our last arguments. It was over something trivial, but in that moment, it felt like the straw that broke the camel's back. We had the same argument for the thousandth time. We'd planned to spend the evening together, just the two of us. I suggested we try the new restaurant downtown, a place with live music and a chef everyone was talking about. Josh shrugged. "Why spend so much when we can just order pizza and watch Netflix?"

I pushed. "It's not just about the food. It's about getting out of the house, experiencing something together. I'm tired of feeling like we're roommates."

His expression darkened; his jaw tightened. "So now I'm not good enough because I don't want to waste money on overpriced pasta?"

"It's not about the money, Josh! It's about doing something… different. You're content with the same routine every day. I'm not. I want more."

"More? What's wrong with what we have?"

I didn't have the words then, but I wasn't happy with what we had. In that moment, I felt the divide between us grow, like a chasm of unmet needs and frustrations we couldn't even speak.

I left to clear my head, telling him I was going to the bookstore. But I didn't go to the bookstore. I just drove around, replaying the same conversations over and over in my head. When I finally returned home, I sat in the driveway, gripping the steering wheel, tears streaming down my face. I couldn't bring myself to go inside, to face the suffocating familiarity of our home. I wasn't angry anymore. I was just… exhausted. We were married, but why did I feel so alone? I travelled alone, which hurt the most, but only because of my expectations. We'd planned trips together, but he'd back out at the last minute. Said he couldn't afford it or couldn't get the time off, valid excuses, sure, but it felt like rejection when they came too late.

It wasn't just about Josh. It was about me. About the fear that I was becoming someone I didn't recognize. I had promised myself, years ago, watching my parents' volatile marriage, that I would never settle for a relationship like theirs. The kind where constant fighting was normal, but no one ever actually communicated. My parents yelled about everything, but when it really mattered, silence was the only answer. I learned to hide my feelings, to resist the urge to cry, to hold everything in.

I remember hearing their arguments as a child, muffled through the walls, sharp enough to make my stomach churn. It was exhausting just to witness, and I promised myself I would never live like that. But now, I wasn't so sure I'd done much better. I had escaped the shouting, but the silence in my relationship was just as deafening.

I didn't want that.

I wanted a partnership. One where we grew together. One where every day felt like the first. Where the effort didn't stop. Where the actions matched the words. Where we woke up and chose each other every day. Even when things got hard. Especially through hard conversations.

I thought wanting more made me selfish. But now, lying in the quiet of my new apartment, I realized it wasn't selfish. This was my life.

He didn't deserve how I treated him toward the end, my radio silence, my unwillingness to try, and how I couldn't express what I was feeling until I finally said those words no one wants to hear: "I want a divorce."

The unsolicited advice from others didn't help either: "You'll work it out. Just give it time." "He doesn't cheat or hit you; why leave?" But none of that mattered. None of it could fix what we were. We were two people growing in opposite directions, and no amount of staying could change that. Just because I was the one who initiated the break-up, it was assumed that I was okay. I was far from okay. I spent my share of time crying into a bottle of wine, throwing pictures at the wall and just being angry at everyone.

There was a time, not too long ago, when I thought maybe selling our house and buying a new one would solve everything. We thought a bigger house, better layout, and larger backyard for the dogs would solve everything. I thought maybe a change of scenery would ease the way I felt. But after looking at several homes and not finding anything we could afford, we put a hold on it.

Deep down, I knew that wasn't the answer. A house wouldn't fix my feelings. It wouldn't change anything. The house didn't need to change. I needed to change. It wasn't the house that was broken, it was me. And it was us. We needed to change how we were living, how we were showing up for each other and for ourselves.

A life untethered from the city and its expectations. A life where I could wake up to something fresh, something unknown.

Something simpler.

I needed change. Not because I was running from something, but because I was finally ready to run toward something else.

So, I left. And never came back.

I thought leaving would be the hardest part.

But the hardest part was facing the person I had become, cleaning up the mess I'd made, and trying to understand how I'd gotten here.

Chapter 2

6 Months Earlier

When I left, I had no plan. No savings. No fallback. I didn't even know where I'd sleep that night. My friend Laura reached out, asking how I was doing. I told her about the separation. She asked where I was staying. I lied and said I had a place lined up or maybe I'd grab a hotel for a few nights. Both sounded just convincing enough. Then she solved at least one of my problems in a single breath.

"John and I are putting our house up for sale soon. Did you want to stay in it, until it sells? We aren't living there right now, and for insurance purposes, we'd feel better having someone stay there." And just like that, I had a roof over my head. Laura didn't know it, but she saved me—caring for me when I couldn't care for myself. Thank God for good people.

It became my place to get drunk and chain-smoke. Alone. Avoid what I needed to face. In the hot tub. Almost every night. I'm sure that's not how she wanted me to use the place. The house, too big for one person, sat in a beautiful part of the city — filled with curated furniture and empty silence. I had everything I needed, everything but peace.

I think about calling Josh. Maybe inviting him over to talk. Am I stupid for walking away from everything I knew? Inviting a soon-to-be ex-husband over for a "talk" in a hot tub? That felt like walking a thin line. But after a few glasses of wine, danger didn't seem so threatening. Honestly, after something strong, I felt like I could do anything. I turn down the Bluetooth speaker perched on the edge of the hot tub and pick up my phone. I hover over Josh's number, torn between loneliness and a quiet tug of regret. I've walked away from the life I knew—the one I thought I wanted—and from the only man I've ever loved.

Was I the biggest idiot in the world? Or just drunk? Probably both. Guilt churns in my chest, mixing with the wine I've made a nightly ritual, the steam rising from the water as clouded as my thoughts. What did I do? Why did I do it? Could we fix this? Am I just scared to be alone? A part of me wanted to slip beneath the water and disappear. The ache was sharp, like grief I hadn't fully accepted. I felt hollow, unmoored. I wanted to call him, apologize, pour my heart out but the words got stuck in my throat. I didn't even know where to begin.

Then, just as I'm spiraling, my friend Kristen's name flashes on my screen—a lifeline, pulling me back from the edge. "Sam, dump the wine and go inside. Sleep it off."

She knows the routine. She knows me. Drinking alone. Regret clinging to me like a second skin. But she didn't know half of it. Kristen was one of my best friends, but I couldn't even let her see what I was becoming. A version of me I didn't even recognize. I wanted to ignore her, but I compromised. I finished the wine, then went to bed. I woke up the next morning feeling two things: relief and regret.

Relief that I didn't do anything stupid. Regret, because... wine.

I drank wine not because I loved it, but because it's all I could afford. It's a cheap stand-in for my old favourite: gin and soda. For under ten bucks, I can avoid the full weight of reality.

I used to be okay. Actually, better than okay. But I never saved anything. I spent like the future wasn't coming. Now it's here, and I'm barely treading water.

Worse? I agreed to keep paying my share of the mortgage... for a house I don't even live in anymore. I'm financially drowning in a life I no longer occupy.

After almost two months of living in Laura's house, I realized that my problems didn't stay in that hot tub but were, rather, packed up like the rest of my stuff.

I force myself to look at my finances.

One account: negative $143.

The other: thirteen cents.

Both credit cards? Maxed.

I'd already borrowed the first and last month's rent from my parents. The shame of needing help to clean up a mess entirely of my own making stung.

I take screenshots of my bank accounts receipts of rock bottom, like I'm archiving my humiliation. Then, instead of dealing with any of it, I open Tinder.

Tinder sounds like a better distraction than my dwindling net worth. The truth is, I'm not ready. Not ready to face the debt, the pain, the heartbreak, the healing. Not ready to own this version of myself. Not yet.

Chapter 3

Alcohol, cigarettes, and red flags disguised as tall, attractive men became my new coping mechanisms. They filled the silence I wasn't ready to sit with and masked the finances I didn't want to face.

First, there was Mark.

I met him through a mutual friend. He was ten years older, very persuasive and also kind, or so I thought. At first, I thought I'd filter out anyone over 35 but maybe I was searching for someone who felt older, grounded, stable. He lived nearly four hours away, yet I made the drive every time. He never came to me.

I convinced myself that if I showed effort, it would turn into something real. But it didn't. Looking back, I didn't know why I had expected it to. It didn't take long to realize he wasn't looking for a relationship—at least, not with me. I thought he would be the one.

Turns out, I was the side chick. He was already engaged to someone who lived across the country.

He let it slip one night. We were out for dinner when his phone kept buzzing, and I finally asked, "Who keeps calling you?" That's when he came clean.

The next morning, while he was still asleep, I deleted his number and walked out without saying goodbye.

Thank you, next.

I only signed up for Tinder because my friend Stacey grabbed my phone and did it for me. One night, while I was sulking over wine and heartbreak, she downloaded the app and made my profile.

At that point, I was more curious than hopeful. I hadn't dated in over 12 years and never through an app. The idea felt foreign and terrifying. I remembered hearing horror stories from friends and once thinking, *Thank God I'd never have to do that.*

Yet here I was, swiping through strangers, looking for a distraction.

I flipped to my profile and reread what it said:

Samantha, 30

I make my money by reading books and sharing what I think about them, recently separated.

And then just one line about what I was looking for:

New to dating, looking for good company.

Truth was, I had no idea what I was looking for or what I wanted.

Then came Adam.

His profile stood out from the endless sea of gym mirror selfies and fish held triumphantly by their gills. One photo showed him on a Sea-Doo, hair wind-whipped, and his bio read: **Lover of adventures, heavy metal music, and a good beer. Age 39.**

He seemed like someone who knew who he was—and I was tired of games. I swiped right. We matched immediately. His first message popped up within minutes:

Adam: So, what's the best road trip you've ever been on?

I stared at the screen for a moment, surprised by the question. Then I typed back:

It wasn't about where we went, but who I was with. A few girlfriends and I drove to Minneapolis when we all turned 21. Five of us crammed into an ancient Honda. Greasy diners, dive bars, dancing to a band we'd never heard of, flirting with guys we'd never see again.

His reply was instant:

Adam: That sounds like the best kind of road trip, the kind that stays with you. Want to grab dinner sometime?

There was something refreshingly direct about him. No pressure. No dragging things out. It was an easy distraction.

We exchanged a few more messages and set a date for the following weekend. He offered to drive to me, three hours without hesitation. That alone felt like a small miracle, considering I'd been the one making all the effort with Mark.

He chose a cozy Italian spot downtown with candlelit tables, soft music, the kind of place I had no business being in, given my financial situation.

He arrived first. As I walked in, he stood to greet me with a warm smile. Something about the way he looked at me made me feel like I'd made the right decision. He was even more handsome in person and rugged; in a way his photos hadn't fully captured. His light brown hair was a little longer, slightly tousled, and he carried himself with an easy confidence.

Dinner was... effortless.

We talked about everything: music, travel, his recent breakup, the contrast between his small-town roots and my city life. He laughed easily, his smile crinkling the corners of his eyes. I found myself leaning in, hanging on every word.

When the check came, he reached for it before I could offer. "I had a really good year and made a lot of money," he joked. "I'm happy to get this one."

The comment caught me off guard. Was he trying to impress me? Or was it just nervous overcompensation? I wasn't sure, but I let it go. As we stepped out into the cool night, I hesitated, unsure whether to invite him back. Before I could decide, he spoke.

"I brought a nice bottle of wine," he said. "Thought maybe we could head back to your place. Talk more. You could tell me more about yourself." His tone was casual, but his eyes held an expectation. I paused. Part of me wanted to say no. The other lonely, flattered, curious part of me wanted the night to stretch just a little longer. I said yes.

Back at my apartment, we sat at the kitchen table. The soft glow from the pot lights cast golden halos on the walls as we sipped our wine. We talked more about families, dreams, regrets. His hand brushed mine, and this time, I didn't pull away.

We kissed. His lips were warm. His touch was confident, but not demanding. For the first time in what felt like forever, I felt something stir inside me, something alive.

The excitement and his dominance were so alluring, I was completely enthralled by his touch.

He stayed the night. Then the night after that. It felt like we were both satisfying a craving we'd carried for too long. It felt like he came over to avoid whatever was at his place and he was the distraction I needed to deal with my internal mess.

We spent hours texting and talking on the phone; his voice quickly became a comfort woven into my days. The following weekend, he made the three-hour drive to see me with flowers in hand and my favourite bottle of wine tucked under his arm. I started to look forward to the sound of his truck pulling into my driveway, the way his presence filled a space I still hadn't learned to call home.

But as much as I enjoyed spending time with Adam, small cracks started to show.

One night, as we sat on the couch scrolling through his phone to pick a playlist, I noticed the photo on his lock screen of the same Seadoo picture from his Tinder profile. Something about it tugged at my attention.

"Wait," I said, laughing. "This is the same picture from your profile. How old is it?" He glanced down and smiled sheepishly. "Oh, that one? A few years ago. It's one of my favourites." "A few years?" I repeated, a flicker of unease rising. "So… how old are you really?" He hesitated. The smile faltered. "I'm 43."

I blinked. "43? Your profile says 39." He ran a hand through his hair and laughed nervously. "Yeah, that was a mistake when I set it up. I never fixed it. Honestly, I didn't think it mattered."

I tried to brush it off, but it gnawed at me. It wasn't just a lie—it was what it said about him. What else was he hiding? Still, I kept seeing him. He felt familiar, and I wanted to believe his intentions were good.

But things added up strangely. He often made comments about money that didn't sit right with me. Since our first dinner, he'd insisted we stay in so we didn't "waste gas" or spend unnecessarily. It didn't make sense especially after telling me how much money he made last year.

Then came the evening everything shifted. New Year's Eve was approaching, and I wanted to spend it with him. I sent a text, securing plans. "I hope I get to be your New Year's kiss…"

Adam: Samantha…

The three little dots appeared…

Adam: I need to tell you something.

My stomach clenched.

What is it?

Adam: There's someone, my ex. We've been talking again. She reached out a few weeks ago and… I think I need to see where it goes.

I stared at the screen, the words hitting like a punch to the gut.

You're kidding, right? I typed. Five minutes passed. The longest five minutes ever.

Adam: I'm sorry. You've been amazing, but I owe it to her to see if there's still something there.

I hope she's worth it, I wrote, feeling something inside me crack.

For weeks, I felt like a fool. The guy who drove hours to see me, who filled my weekends with warmth and laughter, had been holding onto someone else the entire time. It wasn't just that he picked her, it was the feeling of being second. Again.

It hurt but then again, there was a trail of red flags that I kept avoiding.

Fuck him and his bullshit. Hope they live happily ever after. I deleted his number. I was done.

With him.

Then came Jeff, the entrepreneur who loved the sound of his own voice. He was fun but he talked too much about his ex and too much about himself. I don't even think he knew anything about me. Dan, the hockey player who never stayed long enough for anything real. Nice guy - but that was never going to go anywhere. Derek, the master of late-night texts who couldn't hold a conversation in daylight.

Each date blurred into the next small talk over drinks, surface-level connections, a growing realization that I wasn't really looking for them. I was just avoiding myself. It wasn't like me, none of it. The drinking, the hookups, the half-hearted dates, it wasn't who I was. But maybe that was the point.

For so long, I was Josh's girlfriend. Then his wife. I met him young, and he became my world. For years, I didn't know who I was outside of that relationship. These men. Were they even men though? Maybe they were my way of figuring it out or so I told myself. It fed my ego, knowing they wanted me, even if only for a little while.

But it all started to feel repetitive. Shallow. Numbing. Deep down, I knew I needed to get my life together. Maybe I jumped in too soon. Maybe I needed to. The silence scared me more than bad dates. My finances were a mess. I was drowning in emotions I hadn't faced. But instead of dealing with it, I was smoking, drinking, and dating it away, hoping that if I ignored the mess long enough, it would disappear.

Spoiler: it didn't.

Every hangover brought me back to the same unresolved place. The only stable thing in my life was Mischa and the book reviews I took on, both I couldn't afford to screw up. They kept the lights on, food in the fridge and my heart full.

I moved into my apartment just after Christmas, right before New Year's. It felt like the right time to focus not just on unpacking boxes, but on unpacking myself. I told myself I was over it. But my heart didn't get the memo. Just as I was about to delete the app, the Tinder chime echoed.

Jackson, 37. Electrician.

I forgot I'd swiped on him earlier. He reminded me of Dean from Supernatural, but with a beard. Mysterious. Soft eyes. Rugged. His profile mentioned road trips, motorcycles, and whiskey. There was something intriguing about him.

Two photos: one in a sharp navy suit clearly at a wedding. The other holding a Coors Light in front of a fire, his smile backlit by warm flames. Ruggedly handsome. The kind of man who didn't need to try too hard.

He messaged first.

Jackson: 1.5 hours might be a bit of a drive, but I'm thinking you're worth it.

Bold, but not cocky. There was a confidence in his words that made me feel seen.

We'll see about that, won't we? I replied.

Messages flowed easily over the next few days, like we already knew each other. Then he offered to make the drive.

Jackson: No pressure. But I'd love to meet you. I'll bring the whiskey.

Something about him felt…mysterious and kind. I said yes.

I'm not sure why. Maybe I was naïve. Maybe I was just desperate for connection. Or maybe I just didn't care anymore. It didn't feel risky. Except for the possibility of falling in love or the slight chance I'd invited a murderer into my apartment. Either way, it felt like a risk I was willing to take. He couldn't be worse than the others. Unless, of course, he was a murderer.

The night he arrived; my apartment was still in transition. Boxes lined the walls, some spilling their contents. There wasn't much furniture, just my bed. The only thing I'd hung was a wooden frame with a quote I'd found in a rare moment of hope:

You must go on adventures to find out where you truly belong. - Sue Fitzmaurice.

When he knocked, I opened the door to find him holding a bottle of whiskey in one hand, a bottle of wine and a bouquet of red roses in the other. His smile was warm, disarming.

"I wasn't sure what you preferred," he said with a grin. "So, I brought both." I laughed, stepping aside. "Well, now I feel spoiled." "Good," he replied, glancing around. "Looks like you're still settling in." "Yeah, it's a work in progress," I said, gesturing to the chaos. "I like it," he said, setting the bottles on the counter. "Feels real. Like you."

His words caught me off guard. My cheeks warmed. He had a way of making me feel seen—not judged, just understood. We poured drinks and lingered in the kitchen. It was late, around 8:30. In my head, I wondered what his intentions were. I knew mine. But I wasn't ready to say them aloud, not yet.

We talked and laughed. The wine took the edge off my nerves. He told me about his long work hours, fixing things with his hands. I told him about starting over, how this apartment still didn't feel like home. He listened, really listened. His gaze, steady. His questions, sincere.

There was something magnetic about him. An edge, sure. But underneath it, a kindness. By the time the whiskey was halfway gone, it felt like we'd known each other for years. Eventually, the conversation slowed. The air shifted. He brushed a strand of hair from my face. His fingers lingered just long enough to send a shiver down my spine.

"You're beautiful, you know that?" he said softly. Before I could respond, his lips were on mine. Warm. Deliberate. No hesitation. We were all over each other as we stumbled toward my bedroom, the only space that felt remotely put together. The bed was hastily made. A pile of laundry sat in the corner like accidental décor.

It didn't matter. Things were minutes from getting messier anyway. He backed into the room, lay on the bed, then paused. Brushing my hair from my face, he looked into my eyes. "Hey," he said, his voice low. "Can we take a break for a second?" I tilted my head. "Are you okay?"

He nodded, sitting up, running a hand through his hair. "Yeah. I'm okay. It's just…" he hesitated. "I like you. I really like you." He searched for the right words.

"And I don't want this to feel rushed. Or like it's only about… this. You're not just some girl I met. You are someone

I… I've been so excited to get to know. I didn't want to mess it up by rushing into things."

But as soon as he said that, my mind spiraled. He doesn't like me. What did I do wrong? He's not attracted to me. It was such a different reaction than I was used to. The other guys had always wanted more and wanted to take things further, faster. But he didn't.

He was different.

He stayed the night, and we lay in bed talking until the early hours of the morning. After we'd talked for a while, he got up, pulled on his clothes, and told me he'd be back shortly. He came back with coffee and breakfast sandwiches.

He'd noticed the empty kitchen. No food. No coffee. And just like that, he hit my love language without even knowing it.

Chapter 4

Lying in bed now, it feels like I've travelled years emotionally, even though only a few months have passed. Christmas came and went. New Year's was quiet—just a dinner with a few friends and an early night in with Mischa. I couldn't afford much, but I made the best of it. My parents offered to fly me back to Thunder Bay, my childhood home, but I didn't feel up to it. I just wanted to be alone, to start figuring out where my life was going. My parents were always trying to bail me out of whatever disaster I created for myself and I couldn't allow them to anymore. I had to go through it and suffer through the lessons on my own, even being 12 hours away didn't feel like far enough for them to see how far deep I was in.

Jackson and I stayed in touch. On weekends, we took turns making the drive—him to me one week, me to him the next. Each visit felt like an escape from the chaos of reality. He adored me in a way I hadn't felt in years—attentive, thoughtful, always one step ahead of my needs. He'd show up with my favourite snacks, insist on cooking dinner, and pour me a glass of wine before I could protest. And yet, even as we grew close, I sensed him holding back—like he wasn't ready to fully let me in.

When he suggested a weekend away, I was thrilled. "Just us," he said. "No work, no distractions—just you, me, and

Mischa." We booked a cozy cabin halfway between our places. It had a fireplace, a stocked kitchen, everything we needed. It felt like the next step—a chance to deepen what we had.

The first day was perfect. We went for a long walk, laughed, and cooked dinner together. The rhythm between us was easy, natural—like we'd been doing it for years. That night, we poured drinks and settled by the fire, talking about road trips and all the places we still wanted to see.

But as the evening wore on, I noticed his glass never stayed empty. He refilled it again and again, his laughter louder, his body slower. I gently suggested he pace himself, but he waved me off with a grin. "I'm fine," he said, pouring another.

By nine, he was passed out on the couch, the bottle nearly empty beside him.

I sat there for a while, staring at him, disappointment pooling in my chest. This weekend was supposed to be about us—intentional time, building something real. Instead, I was alone. Cleaning up the bottles. Sitting in silence. Thank God I'd brought Mischa. At least I wasn't completely alone. She stayed beside me the whole night; it was like she knew I needed her comfort. It wasn't that she didn't like Jackson, but I don't think she sensed stability with him. She allowed him to be close but she kept her distance and didn't go out of her way to get more of his attention.

The next morning, he woke up groggy and apologetic, mumbling something about getting carried away. I nodded, not trusting myself to speak. I wanted to believe it was a one-time thing. But deep down, I knew better. Because the second night was a carbon copy of the first.

On the drive back to his place, the silence was deafening. When we pulled into his driveway, he leaned over to kiss me goodbye and I let him, even though I knew it would be the last time. Mischa immediately hopped in the front seat, curled up in her donut shape and closed her eyes.

As I drove away, tears blurred my vision. I wasn't ready to let him go. But I had to. I couldn't ignore the truth: Jackson wasn't ready to let me in and no matter how much I cared, I couldn't make him. He was like a tall glass of whiskey—intoxicating, warm, and just dangerous enough to burn. And that burn had become too much.

His behaviour reflected back to me how I had been living. It was a reminder of what I needed to change.

When I got back to my apartment, I looked around—the half-unpacked boxes still sitting there, taunting me. Part of me felt like if I unpacked, it meant I'd truly committed to being here. I had poured so much of myself into Jackson, into us—and for what? A bottle of whiskey and a passed-out man during a weekend meant for connection?

I felt foolish. Exhausted. Like I'd betrayed the part of me that had promised to do better. I wasn't heartbroken—I was angry. At myself. How did I let this happen again? How did I get so wrapped up in someone else's potential, in their charm, their promises?

I still had so much of my own life to untangle. And the spark I'd been chasing, the one that would shake me awake and make me feel alive again—still wasn't there. Then it hit me: maybe I couldn't attract someone whole if I didn't feel whole.

I couldn't meet my king if I hadn't become my own queen.

I was broke, relying on credit cards and my next paycheck. I could barely afford extras like coffee or a new top. My life was messy, uncertain, and loaded with emotional baggage, so of course, I was attracting guys who were just as emotionally unavailable.

I had been judging him for not having his life together, but I was nowhere near having mine together either. I was drinking too much. Avoiding my own life. Just like he was. He wasn't to blame. None of them were.

They were nothing more than mirrors. And lessons.

Each time, it felt like the guy would get my hopes up, only to let me down or I'd come to realize how mismatched we were. Most of them were fresh out of breakups or breaking down in some way, and really, we were just filling voids. One disappointment bled into the next: I was clinging to the idea that someone else could fill a space only I was meant to fill.

I needed to be single. Really single. Because I'd never given myself that chance to discover who I was without molding myself to someone else's expectations. Being alone didn't have to feel like punishment. Maybe it could be the greatest gift I'd ever give myself.

The one I really needed to date was me.

I was long overdue for a reality check. I couldn't wake up hungover one more time. My days of blacking out, waking up in someone else's bed, and questioning my morals were over. I was tired of crying over people who saw me as an option. Tired of feeling like a second choice. I told myself I was only using them to feel wanted. But maybe, deep down, I wanted to be chosen for real.

But underneath all that disappointment, there was something else, a quiet ember that hadn't gone out. For the first time in a long time, I had let myself feel something real. I'd opened my heart bruised, fragile, but open—and that counted for something. Jackson had reminded me that love, messy and imperfect as it is, was still possible. He showed me I could care deeply. That I could be vulnerable again, even if it didn't last.

Maybe dating hadn't been about finding the one, but about becoming the one, the version of myself that attracted what I truly deserved. Jackson wasn't a turning point, he was part of the pattern.

But I had work to do. My life was still a mess: my closet, my bank account, my apartment. I needed to unpack. Emotionally. Mentally. Financially. Physically. Just as I started to feel the flicker of a new beginning, my phone pinged with a text message.

Adam. The one who left me for his ex.

Adam: Hey. Been thinking about you. Can we talk?

I shoot back the quickest reply. *About what?*

Adam: Any chance I could see you next weekend?

Why? I was already annoyed.

Adam: I'm sorry about how I left things last time. I made a mistake.

Let me guess things didn't work out with your ex?

Adam: No, they didn't. I'm sorry I made you feel like you weren't enough. I messed up. Can we talk? Can I see you?

For a second, I considered it. The chemistry was still there—the pull, undeniable. But then I remembered the nights I spent piecing myself back together. The promises I'd made to myself.

I appreciate you saying that, I replied, voice steady. *But I can't do this again.*

He never replied. And I didn't reach out either. I deleted the app, erased the numbers I'd saved, and got a gym membership.

The next few months were about me. I poured into the life I was building, quiet, intentional, mine. Mischa was my constant companion. I started fixing the financial mess I'd ignored for too long, took on more client work, and even began moonlighting as a delivery driver for one of my favourite restaurants just to make some extra money.

I found peace in the in-between the strange limbo of leaving behind a life that no longer fit and slowly crafting one that felt like mine. It was calm, but uncertain. Like waiting for a new chapter to begin. I was ready for a big change.

Even if things weren't perfect, they were taking shape. Less chaos. More clarity. My routine was stable. I wasn't scrambling every month to pay rent. I kept my social circle small. Still stayed off the apps. And slowly, I started to feel better, more like someone I actually recognized. Then, one night, just as the quiet wrapped around me like a blanket, my phone chimed. Facebook Messenger.

My stomach fluttered—an involuntary response I didn't want to name. I set the book down in my lap, heart thudding as I reached for my phone. Mischa's head rested on my legs, warm and heavy—a reminder to breathe.

I didn't know why I felt nervous. But maybe I did. I swiped open the app. My thumb hovered over the message icon. And then I saw it.

James. A name I hadn't seen in over a decade.
A name I hadn't seen in over a decade.
A name that still held weight.
A name that carried history.

James: Hey Sam, I know it's been like a decade since we spoke or seen each other but I randomly came across a song that reminded me of you from when we used to hang out. I looked through your pictures, still looking as good as I remember. How's it going?

Chapter 5

I Think It Was Like 15 Years Ago…

If I had to sum up that New Year's Eve in 2004 with a single word, it would be mortifying. If it were a book or a movie, I'd give it one star: poorly developed characters, rushed pacing, and a climax that fell flat literally and figuratively. And yet, like all bad stories, it clung to me. I couldn't stop thinking about it. I needed closure. I needed to know how it ended.

Everyone remembers their first time. It's one of those sticky, permanent memories you can't seem to scrape off. And yet, I think most people would gladly forget theirs if they could. I know I would.

I wish I could forget how painfully awkward and entirely unromantic it was. Why do we glorify this moment? Why do we build it up like it's some glittering milestone, when most of the time, it's clumsy, disappointing, and soaked in regret? We're sold this fantasy of candles, rose petals, soft music, slow, tender love. You wake up in their arms, blissfully tangled, a perfect beginning to forever.

Sorry to ruin it for you, but that's not how it usually goes. No one tells you the truth: your first time probably won't be good. You won't enjoy it, not really. You think you did, but only because you had nothing else to compare it to.

That night felt like the beginning of everything. Or at least, I wanted it to be. Looking back, maybe it didn't change anything at all. And maybe that was part of the heartbreak.

It was one of those brutally cold nights when the air slices against your skin like tiny knives. But inside the cabin, it was warm and buzzing, hazy with bodies and cheap liquor. The alcohol made me feel loose, wrapped me in a dull, fuzzy kind of courage. I don't remember the outside of the cabin, just the faint image of an outhouse by the front door and acres of land swallowed by darkness. We'd arrived late, and when I stumbled out the next morning, I was too eager to disappear to take in any real details.

I'd gone with a group of friends, one of whom was dating the guy who owned the place. Or maybe his parents did. I didn't care. I wasn't there for the party or the people or the midnight countdown. I was there for James.

I knew he'd be there. That was all it took to send me spiraling into a flurry of anxious preparation, trying to look effortless, trying to feel confident, and praying, silently, just to be seen.

James had that way about him. He didn't have to try. He just was. Effortless. Magnetic. I, on the other hand, needed help. By "help," I mean liquid armor. I wasn't the kind of girl who felt at ease at parties. I hadn't dated much. Flirting was a language I hadn't learned yet. But after a few drinks, I didn't care how inexperienced I was. Or maybe I just stopped noticing.

The cabin was crammed with people and noise. The air was thick with the scent of sweat, cheap perfume, and something sour under the surface. Top 40 hits blasted from tiny speakers, and I held my drink like a lifeline, eyes scanning the room.

I was waiting for him to see me. And when I did finally catch his eye, I also noticed there weren't any other girls around. Not available ones, anyway. Just me.

He made you feel like you were the only person in the room. Even if it was just for five minutes. Maybe I was the only one left. Maybe everyone else had already paired off, wandered off, or passed out. Either way, in that moment, it felt like it was just me and him.

He was never the guy who'd choose me over someone else—he was the guy who chose me when no one else was around. I'd accepted that truth a long time ago. But that night? That night, it didn't seem to matter.

He smiled at me from across the room, his eyes lingering just long enough to make my heart stutter. For a moment, it felt like he'd chosen me before I even walked through the door. The way he looked at me made me feel wanted. Actually wanted.

"Samantha," he said as he finally came over, his voice low and warm, his arm brushing mine like an afterthought. "You look... amazing." I laughed—too loud, too eager. "Thanks. You don't look too bad yourself."

We spent the night talking, drinking, orbiting closer with every hour. When the countdown to midnight began echoing through the cabin, we were already kissing. And when the clock struck 12, he leaned in again—his lips brushing mine with the kind of confidence that comes with either experience or just too much alcohol.

It didn't feel magical or cinematic. It felt rushed. Clumsy. But I didn't care. I was finally the girl James wanted. Somehow, we ended up in one of the bedrooms upstairs. The details are fuzzy now a mix of nerves, inexperience, and too much vodka. I remember fumbling with buttons, his hands warm against my skin, and the way I convinced myself this is how it's supposed to happen.

The music was blaring downstairs. I could barely hear myself think and maybe that was for the best. No thoughts. Just instinct. Just going with it. There were no candles, no deep eye contact, no tender intimacy—just motion and detachment. Just wham, bam, thanks and see you never again.

I woke up the next morning mortified. Alone. Head pounding. Stomach tight with regret. All I wanted was to disappear. But I couldn't. I still had to go downstairs and find a way home. At first, I questioned if it had even happened. But the dull ache in my body and the hollow throb in my chest told me it had.

I gathered my clothes from the floor, got dressed as fast as I could, and tiptoed downstairs, hoping no one would be around. But everyone was there. Everyone. Or at least it felt that way. And they were staring. Laughing. Mortified doesn't even cover it.

At that moment, I hated everyone. My shame felt like it had a pulse. I found my friend Kristen and asked if I could take her car back into town. She said yes and said she'd grab a ride with someone else. Thank God for good friends.

I never heard from James again. Not that day. Not that week. Not for years. No call. No text. No "Hey, how are you?" Not even a thumbs-up emoji. We stayed friends on Facebook. I saw his posts, his pictures, the life he was living in a world that had nothing to do with mine. But not once did he acknowledge what happened.

To be fair, I never reached out either. What would I even say? For almost fifteen years, I carried that night like a stone in my chest. Not because I still wanted him—but because I never understood why. Why did he choose me? And why it meant so little to him… when it had meant so much to me.

Now, staring at his name in my DMs, I felt that familiar weight shift in my chest—a stone pressing harder against my ribs. After all this time. After all these years of silence. There he was. Back.

And for the first time in nearly fifteen years, I let myself wonder: Was I ready to face him? To face the part of myself I thought I'd buried?

Back then, James had felt like the pinnacle of my peak, the best I could ever hope for. But life, in its relentless way, kept moving. It dragged me along, reshaping me in the process. Somewhere in the chaos, I met someone who redefined what love could look like.

That someone was Josh.

He was nothing like James. Where James was bold and magnetic, Josh was quiet, steady. He didn't sweep me off my feet; he stood beside me. Grounded me in a way I hadn't known I needed. With him, I felt seen not for what I could offer, but for who I was. That alone felt revolutionary.

For a long time, that was enough.

Even though Josh wasn't my first, in many ways, he made me feel like he was. Part of me wishes I had waited just a little longer so he could have been. I rejected him at first. Not because of who he was, but because I didn't yet know how to accept the kind of love he offered. There were no games. No chasing. He wanted me, and he showed it. And that terrified me. The ease of it was unfamiliar. Uncomfortable, even.

Still, James's shadow never fully disappeared. He remained a lingering "what if," a question mark at the edge of memory. Sometimes I'd catch myself wondering how different things might've been if we'd ever had our chance. If that night had meant something more if it hadn't turned into a memory I winced every time it surfaced. Would we have worked? Would he have been good for me? Or would I have spent years chasing the same empty validation I once craved, confusing longing with love?

Now, here he was again. A message. A name lighting up my phone. A ghost, suddenly solid. And I couldn't help but feel the pull.

That New Year's Eve felt like yesterday. Yet it was a lifetime ago. I was eighteen, young, uncertain, and reaching for meaning in all the wrong places. I thought James's attention would fix something in me, fill in the hollowness, prove that I was worth choosing.

But my life has changed. I've changed. Since that girl in the cabin, I've loved and lost, built and rebuilt. I've fallen hard and learned how to get back up—alone. And still, James showing up now feels like the universe asking a question. Daring me to look back. To consider what might have been. To wonder what might still be.

Or maybe it was a test. A quiet whisper from fate asking: Are you still that same girl? The one waiting to be chosen?

Chapter 6

For years, I had been building a life inside these four walls, brick by careful brick. But lately, it felt like I'd locked myself in. The sound of traffic and constant sirens that once energized me now just irritated me.

There was a time I craved the city—the bustle, the noise, the endless movement.

Now it all felt suffocating. Mechanical. Like I was just going through the motions.

The routines that once grounded me now smothered me.

I couldn't pinpoint when it had started, this longing for something else—something quieter, simpler. Something that didn't feel like the same old weight of familiarity but instead, the lightness of possibility.

But it wasn't just about James. It was about me. About the life I wanted. And the courage it would take to claim it.

Maybe I wasn't searching for closure with James after all. Maybe I was looking for a reason to let go of the past—to finally untangle myself from it. Reconnecting with him wasn't about rekindling something; it was about daring myself to imagine a life beyond this one.

As Mischa stretched at my feet, her soft sigh filling the quiet of the room, I felt it—a small shift inside me. A flicker of hope. Maybe this was the first step toward change: a conversation, a moment of courage, a willingness to see where it might lead.

And maybe, just maybe, the next step would be leaving this city behind and finding a place where I could feel alive again. A place where I could slow down and finally catch up to the life I knew I was meant to live.

I didn't know where it would take me, but one thing was clear: I couldn't stay here. Not like this. Not when I finally understood I was ready for more.

Chapter 7

I walk Mischa every day. Some days, I really don't want to—when I'm too busy, too tired, or the weather's just miserable. But we go anyway. It's like this unspoken promise I've made, not just to her but to myself. Lately, it feels like the only thing keeping me grounded. The rhythm of her paws on the pavement gives me a strange, quiet peace, like I can finally breathe a little easier, even when my mind refuses to settle. These walks have become my therapy sessions—except I don't speak, and Mischa looks at me like she understands every thought, every fear, every doubt. Maybe she does.

I didn't realize how important these walks were until one day, when we bumped into a man who stopped to admire Mischa, something that happens often. He told me that his dog, Carter, was 17 and the secret to his longevity was a daily walk. "Walk, every day," he said, nodding like he knew something I didn't. I'll never forget that conversation. Since then, I've never missed a day. No matter what, we go.

I'm trying to remind myself that building a better life doesn't happen overnight. It's not about grand gestures or dramatic changes, it's about showing up, even when it feels impossible. Especially when it feels impossible. That's where I struggle. Some days, I feel like I'm moving in circles, stumbling over the same hard lessons again and again. Falling for people who can't love me the way I deserve. Chasing the "what ifs" instead of facing the "what is." It's exhausting.

Walking Mischa, I think about these things a lot. Why do I crave the summit when I'm not willing to take the climb? These questions swirl around in my head, but I don't have all the answers. What I do know, after everything I've been through, is that I need to use my voice. I've kept too much bottled up inside, waiting for someone to treat me the way I deserve. But now I know I need to define what that looks like and stand firm in it. I'm tired of feeling stuck. Tired of repeating the same mistakes.

And then, out of nowhere, James walks back into my life. Like he's been waiting just offstage for the perfect moment to reappear. I haven't seen or heard from him since that reckless New Year's Eve when I was 18. He left shortly after, moving to the other side of the country, as if our story had ended before it even began.

James was my high school crush—not that we went to the same school. I was a teenager, still figuring out who I was, and he was a few years older, orbiting just outside my world but somehow always pulling me into his gravity. We met through mutual friends, and from the start, he stood out as the kind of guy who glowed under a spotlight only he could create.

He had that effortless charm, the kind that made people lean in a little closer, laugh a little louder, just to keep his attention. And sure, he was good-looking, tall, athletic, with a boyish grin that made you feel like the only person in the room. But it wasn't just that. James had a way of making anyone feel special, even if only for five fleeting seconds… and then he'd move on, like it never happened.

And me? I was a good friend. The reliable one. The girl he called when another girl didn't text back. I wasn't the type he chased; those girls had long, tanned legs, glossy blonde hair, and bodies built for bikinis and billboards. They belonged in the kind of stories he wanted to tell.

I was average height, curvy, with dark, pin-straight brunette hair and a laugh people said was warm. I wasn't someone that guys bragged about dating; I was the one they confided in. And I convinced myself that was enough. Being near James even if it meant being his emotional backup felt better than not being near him at all.

Still, every time he fell for someone new, a quiet pang twisted in my chest. A reminder of where I really stood. On the sidelines. The last resort he still somehow made time for.

"So, what happened with your last relationship?" I typed, fingers hesitating above the keyboard before hitting send. I already knew part of the story, but I wanted to hear it from him—raw and unfiltered.

There was a pause. Longer than usual.

James: It's… a lot. But the short version is, she cheated on me.

A dull ache settled in my chest. Sympathy, anger both for him. *James, I'm so sorry. That's awful.*

James: It was a couple years ago now. We were together for almost seven years. I thought we were solid. Then, one day, she just... left. Out of nowhere.

I stared at the screen, the words sitting heavy in the silence. *That must've been devastating,* I wrote, heart breaking a little more with each message.

James: It was. We built a life together. I was blindsided. And then, just like that, she was gone.

I could imagine him snapping his fingers. "She was gone."

James: What made it worse? I saw her with him—her new guy—a couple of weeks later. Ran into them at a coffee shop.

I swallowed hard.

God, James… The words caught in my throat even as I typed them. That's unimaginable.

James: It felt like a punch to the gut. I just stood there. Frozen. Watching them. I couldn't believe how fast she moved on. It made me question everything, every kiss, every memory. I started to wonder if it was all just one big lie.

You didn't deserve that. I typed, my fingers trembling slightly. *Her actions don't define you—they define her.*

James: It took me a long time to get that. To stop blaming myself and wondering what I did wrong. The truth is, I'll probably never get the answers I want. I've had to make peace with the fact that some people just aren't who you thought they were.

I let his words settle into the quiet between us.

You're a good man, James. The right person will see that and show up for you the way you deserve. And maybe I didn't know for sure if he was—but I believed he could be.

James: You think so?

A note of vulnerability threading through his usual confidence.

I know so. I wrote. And for what it's worth, I'm glad you're here, talking to me.

James: Me too. It's been a long time since I've felt this comfortable with someone. Thank you for that.

Later that night, the conversation shifted. James turned the lens on me.

James: So, what about you? How's life post-separation? You're not divorced yet, right? How's that going?

I paused, fingers hovering over the keys. It wasn't easy to admit. But something about James—his openness, the ease between us—made me feel safe enough to be real.

No, not legally divorced yet. It's been… a process. I finally replied. When I left Josh, I didn't just walk away from a relationship. I walked away from the stability we'd built. And into a financial disaster. Most of it was my own doing.

James: What kind of mess?

A big one, I thought. But instead, I type: *Debt. A lot of it is credit cards, personal loans. You name it. I was barely staying afloat, and when I left, I didn't have enough income to keep going. I'm still paying for half the mortgage, on top of this apartment. I almost filed for bankruptcy but ended up submitting a consumer proposal instead.* There was a brief pause.

James: I've been there.

My fingers stilled. *You have?*

James: Well, sort of yeah. A few years ago, I was drowning financially. I came close to bankruptcy too. It messes with your head, doesn't it? Makes you second-guess everything. I never filed anything official, but I had to climb out of a hole. Things turned around eventually.

That surprised me. *You seem like you've got it all together now.*

James: I don't know about that. I borrowed money from my parents to stay above water. Paid them back little by little. After Erika left, it was hard to juggle everything on my own. I didn't realize how much I'd been leaning on the dual income until it was just me left holding the bag.

Honestly, I don't believe in the whole '50/50' thing, I typed. When I was with Josh, we didn't do it that way. I made more money, so I paid most of the bills. And I didn't mind—at least not at first because I thought that's what you do in a partnership. You find your balance, and it's not always about money. Sometimes it's emotional labour. Sometimes it's who's walking the dog, or doing the dishes, or just showing up when life punches you in the gut.

I hesitated, then added:

The problem wasn't money, it was effort. By the end, I was carrying all of it. Financially, emotionally. I didn't even realize how much it was draining me until I finally let it go. But part of that's on me. I never told him how heavy it had gotten.

I sat back and re-read what I'd written, a familiar knot tightening in my stomach. Part of me wondered if I'd said too much again. But another part of me felt a quiet relief. It was the truth, and I'd spent too much of my life burying that. Before I could talk myself out of it, I hit send.

James: Yeah, I get it. But honestly? It kind of sounds like you let yourself get walked all over. I mean, sure, every relationship is different, but don't you think you should've drawn the line somewhere? Like, if you're carrying most of the weight, isn't that more enabling than supporting? I don't know, maybe it's just me, but it sounds like you let it get way out of hand. Wouldn't it have been smarter to set boundaries from the start?

The words hit harder than I expected. They didn't land as concern or curiosity—they landed as judgment, plain and sharp. My stomach twisted. I re-read the message, hoping I'd misunderstood, but no. The assumption was there, glaring and unmissable: that he would've handled it better. That I was the one who failed.

I swallowed the lump rising in my throat.

Yeah. I wrote back eventually. *I had so much love for him. I really thought things would change. I wanted them to. But everything got so heavy, I just… collapsed under it all and I didn't know how to communicate that. I made mistakes. I know that. But all I can do now is learn.*

His reply came quickly, almost too quickly.

James: Exactly. At least you're learning. Some people never do.

I couldn't tell if I felt comforted or condemned. Vulnerability had felt safe with James only minutes ago. Now it felt like walking barefoot over glass. Still, I thanked him for listening and ended the conversation soon after, carrying an uneasy mix of connection and disquiet.

Later that night, lying in bed, I re-read our messages, unsure of what lingered more, the hope or the caution. He wasn't just the charming guy from my past anymore; he was someone who had supposedly been through the fire. But part of me wondered: was there more to his story than he was letting on? Was I falling for the idea of him, rather than the truth of him?

Maybe this wasn't a second chance. Maybe it was our first. A crush that never had a chance to bloom, just one of those fleeting almost that follow you quietly through the years. We always had fun together, and right now, fun and an old friend sounded like exactly what I needed.

That New Year's Eve felt like a shift. Or at least, I wanted to believe it was. When he kissed me, I fell into that hopeful, painfully naïve space where everything means something. I thought maybe, just maybe he was finally seeing me. Not as the backup or the reliable friend, but as someone worth choosing. Worth wanting.

We were both drunk, but we knew what we were doing. Maybe it was the safety he gave me, maybe it was the years of unspoken what-ifs. I don't regret that night—I never did.

But the next morning? Nothing. No calls. No texts. Just silence. A vacuum where possibility used to be.

I replayed every second of that night for weeks, dissecting moments, searching for signs that it had mattered to him. But deep down, I already knew what I was: a moment. Convenient. Disposable. Forgettable.

I knew his type was perfect on the surface, emotionally shallow beneath. And I was never going to be perfect. I never wanted to be. Still, some reckless, tender part of me had believed—for that one wild night that maybe I could be enough. For him. For anyone.

I thought about him over the years more often than I liked to admit. And now, fifteen years later, it felt like we were dusting off the memory of that night, seeing if it still fit. The late-night messages started out playful, but eventually they turned intimate unguarded. We told each other things we hadn't even said to ourselves.

One night, our conversation drifted from childhood memories to the present, and I finally asked the question that had been quietly burning inside me for years.

I had to know.

My fingers hovered for a second before I grabbed my phone and tapped on his name.

Hey. Random question.

James: Ok, shoot!

I'm... curious. About something.

James: Okay, hit me.

That night. New Year's Eve. The cabin. 2004.

James: …Wow. That's not where I thought this was going. What about it?

Why didn't you say anything after? Like, nothing. No call, no message, not even a "Hey, thanks for the awkward night."

James: You're really not going to let me off the hook here, huh?

Nope. I've waited almost fifteen years for an answer. Might as well get one now.

James: Fair. Honestly? I don't know if I have a good answer. I was... scared, I guess.

Scared? Of what?

James: Of messing things up. Of you hating me. Of saying the wrong thing and making it worse. I thought if I just didn't say anything, it would all... disappear.

Oh, so your brilliant plan was to ghost me and hope I'd forget? Bold strategy.

James: I know. It sounds awful. And it was awful. I was young, stupid, and completely unequipped for anything real. Sam, I liked you so much back then I just didn't know how to say it. You were the girl I didn't want to hurt. And I didn't trust myself not to hurt you.

Wait. What? You liked me? Like... liked me liked me?

James: Yes. Why is that so surprising to you?

Umm, I don't know, maybe because you used to flirt with every other girl in the room? Or how I was always your last resort for hangouts?

James: Sam, I was terrified of ruining what we had. I thought our friendship was the best thing in my life. And I didn't want to mess it up by asking you out and getting rejected.

I stared at the screen, stunned. How did he not know I had the world's biggest crush on him? I thought it was obvious. I was sure someone in our friend group had told him. Everyone knew. And if he liked me back... why didn't I know? Why wasn't it obvious?

Me? Reject you? James, I would've done anything just to be with you back then.

But life has a funny way of moving forward especially when you think it can't. Back then, James felt like the pinnacle of everything I could ever hope for. My big what-if. My maybe-forever.

But time dragged me along anyway. And somewhere in that messy middle, I met someone who taught me what real love looked like. Talking to James again felt like stepping into a time machine. It was both thrilling and strange like stumbling across an old song on a dusty mix CD. Familiar. Wistful. Dangerous. Still, every night, I'd lie in bed with a quiet smile, reading his latest message. That bittersweet blend of nostalgia and hope tightened something inside my chest. And I couldn't shake the question: Am I seeing the truth? Or just what I want to see?

Maybe just maybe reconnecting with him wasn't random. Maybe it was leading me to something unexpected. To something real. To the answers I didn't even know I still needed. Maybe... this would be the fairytale ending I had been waiting for. The one I'd dreamed of. Where my first... would be my last.

Chapter 8

The house is gone. Well, not gone—someone else owns it now. Someone else will hang their keys on the little hook by the door, maybe repaint the kitchen cupboards, or finally renovate the bathroom, just as we once planned. The lawyer handed me a check for $2,500 and a stack of paperwork. I walked out of that office feeling like I was carrying a ghost in my purse.

The money was already spoken for. It went toward joint bills, the mortgage, and that was it. I planned to pay my dad back the $2,000 I owed for first and last month's rent, and hang onto the last $500. I drove straight to the lake after. I didn't even get out. Just sat there with the window cracked open, breathing in the cool air, letting it all hit me. And I cried. Not a quiet, movie-scene cry. The kind that folds you in half. The kind that makes your ribs ache.

I don't even know why, exactly, I just couldn't stop. It was everything I'd been holding in. The relief. The grief. The guilt. The guilt over not feeling more grief. Letting go of the house meant letting go of the story I'd clung to, that if I just worked harder, gave more, tried one more time, I could've saved us. But there's nothing left to save. Just me.

When the tears finally stopped, I looked in the rearview mirror, dabbed my eyes with a Kleenex, and drove to therapy.

I've been going once every three weeks since I left Josh. It's the only standing appointment I never cancel.

My therapist is soft-spoken but sharp. She doesn't coddle. She asks the kind of questions that make silence stretch until it aches. Like she holds a mirror to me, not to judge, but to make me look. It's painful. But when I leave, I feel lighter. Clearer.

"I want to ask you something," she said after I finished rambling about my budget spreadsheet and how I'm trying to cook more at home. "Okay," I said, picking at the frayed edge of my sleeve. "What do you think are your core values?" I blinked. "Like… honesty? Loyalty? Respect? I don't know."

She nodded. "Those are a good start. But think about it this way, what values do you live by? What are the non-negotiables for how you want to show up in the world and in your relationships?" I paused. She continued, "When relationships fall apart, it's often not because there wasn't love. It's because their values were misaligned." And here I thought I was emotionally stable today.

All this time, I'd been thinking we just broke. That I wasn't enough. That he didn't try hard enough. But what if we were never even speaking the same language? I stared out the window. "I value growth. Depth. Curiosity," I whispered. "And do you think Josh shared those?"

I didn't answer right away. My mind flooded with memories—unpaid bills, me reading relationship books while he scrolled car forums. Him shutting down anytime I brought up the future. Me always reaching, him always retreating.

"No," I finally said. "He valued… stability. Comfort. Familiarity. He didn't want to change. And I kept trying to drag him with me. We weren't going in the same direction." My voice cracked. I didn't try to hide it.

"It's okay," she said gently. "You weren't wrong for wanting what you wanted. You just wanted it with the wrong person. Not because you weren't good for each other, but because over time, your values changed. You changed."

It's been 47 days since my last drink. 33 since I quit smoking.

I haven't told many people. I don't want the questions or the praise or the expectations. But it's happening. Quietly. Steadily. One day at a time. I've replaced wine with lemon water. Cigarettes with gym sessions. Chaos with routine. I don't always love it but I never regret it.

Breaking habits that once felt like comfort is harder than I expected. They were there for me when no one else was. So, every morning, I say to myself: Today, I am choosing not to drink and not to smoke. And for now, that's enough.

Tonight, I made dinner after walking Mischa—a full meal: grilled chicken with steamed broccoli. I seasoned the chicken with garlic and rosemary, the way my mom used to, and for the first time in a long while, it tasted like care. I ate slowly, at the table, without scrolling on my phone. Mischa lay at my feet, her big brown eyes tracking my every move.

Afterward, we curled up on the couch—me still in damp gym clothes, her head resting on my lap like always. My legs ached, but my heart felt... quiet. In a good way. This was how most nights looked lately. Staying in. Being still. Making room for the quiet. It wasn't easy to find peace in a triplex on a noisy city street—but if we tried hard enough, we could create it. And I'd started to enjoy that. The quiet.

James texted earlier. Just a random nerd emoji. I smiled, sent back a laughing one, and that was it. No heavy conversation. No unraveling. Just something light. For once, he wasn't at the centre of my thoughts. That was new.

I opened my journal and wrote: *Today was simple. Today was clean. I didn't chase, or explain, or beg anyone to understand me. I fed myself. I moved my body. I stayed sober. I walked Mischa.*

Maybe healing doesn't always look like epiphanies. Maybe it looks like eating a meal you made yourself and realizing you don't need a glass of wine just to sit in your own quiet.

I closed the journal and leaned back, letting Mischa's slow, steady breathing lull me into stillness. She'd been with me through everything—every heartbreak, every breakdown, every shaky restart. Somehow, she always knew when I needed her most. I stroked her fur and whispered, "We're doing okay, aren't we?"

She didn't stir. Just let out a deep, contented sigh. And that was all the answer I needed. Still, even in this calm, feet firmer on the ground than they'd been in months, I couldn't silence the question lingering at the edges: What if James isn't just a distraction? What if there's actually something real there?

I used to believe I deserved a fairy tale ending. After everything I'd been through, I needed to know if this connection was genuine—or just nostalgia, dressed up as a second chance. Had he come back because I was finally ready for this kind of love?

James filled the quiet spaces in my day, his messages a soft hum in the background. They comforted me. But part of me still wondered if he was just another Adam or Jackson in disguise—just another mirage keeping me from doing the deeper work I knew I had to do.

For now, it worked. Our conversations didn't demand too much. They gave me a sense of companionship without expectation. It was convenient, in a way that felt manageable. Still, I caught myself wondering what it might be like if he weren't so far away. Then again, maybe distance is what made this feel so easy. For now, I could hold the comfort without letting it consume me.

And for now, that was enough. But James's shadow lingered in the back of my mind, a "what if" that wouldn't fully fade. I found myself drifting into the past, wondering what might've been if that night between us had led somewhere real instead of becoming a memory I still cringe at.

I used to think timing was everything—that we missed our chance because we weren't ready for each other. But now, staring at his message, I wondered if the timing wasn't about missing the moment. Maybe it was about finding your way back when you'd finally grown enough to hold it. Was I ready?

Part of me wanted to ignore him—to leave the past in the past and keep walking forward. But another part, the one that remembered the way his smile once made my heart race, wanted to believe he'd changed too. That I had changed enough.

I took a deep breath, fingers hovering above the keyboard. Maybe the only way to get clarity was to face it head-on. To face him. But was that even possible? Could I actually look James in the eyes after all these years? Did I even have enough credit left to book a flight across the country?

Probably not. But I'd figure it out. I had to. I needed to know. "Am I being stupid, Meesch?" I looked at her, hoping for a sign, some kind of approval. "Shake your head. Give me a high five. Something."

She didn't budge, curled into her usual donut shape on the couch, fast asleep. Mischa usually had a way of sensing my chaos, of offering just enough presence to steady me. But tonight, it felt like she was leaving it up to me. Maybe that was the point.

I should run this by James first. Maybe he wouldn't even like the idea. Maybe he wasn't ready. Maybe he wouldn't be home. At least then I'd know. I grabbed my phone, thumb hesitating above his name. Before I could overthink it again, I tapped. The chat window opened.

What would you say if I came to see you?

My heart hammered in my chest as I hit send. I stared at the screen, breath caught, waiting for the familiar three dots to appear. They did.

James: Wow, that's... shiit. Are you serious?

Yeah. Why not? We've got fifteen years of catching up to do, don't we? The dots danced again. My chest tightened.

James: We do. But is that really what you want? Or are you just chasing some old dream?

I froze. His words landed harder than I expected—sharp, precise, like he'd aimed them at the part of me that was already unsure. Was he questioning me, or trying to protect himself?

What's that supposed to mean?

James: It means... I don't want you to regret it. Sometimes the past is better left where it is, you know?

A knot coiled in my stomach. Was this his version of a soft, no? Or was he afraid of what it could mean if we looked backward too long?

So, what are you saying? That I shouldn't come? The pause dragged. When his reply finally came, it walked a tightrope between hope and hesitation.

James: I'm saying, if you come, it should be because you're ready for whatever happens. Not because you're hoping for something that might not exist anymore.

Cryptic. Maddeningly so. Was he protecting me or preparing to run?

And what about you? Are you ready for whatever happens? His reply was almost instant.

James: I've been ready for years, Sam.

I stared at the words, breath held. Was this an invitation—or a test? A bridge to cross or a final door gently closing?

Mischa stirred at my feet, stretched out her little legs, and yawned. Her sleepy glance felt grounding, like a reminder: whatever this was, reunion, reckoning, restart, I'd come too far to back down now. I took another breath, fingers trembling as I typed:

I'll let you know when I book the flight. As I hit send, something shifted inside me. It wasn't just his name lighting up the screen, it was something deeper.

A restlessness I hadn't been able to name until now. For years, I told myself I wanted stability. Success. A purpose that made sense in a city built on ambition.

But sitting here, in the place I once called home, I felt… nothing. No spark. No thrill. Just the quiet ache of knowing this city no longer held what I was searching for. Maybe it never did.

I looked out the window at the skyline that used to make me feel alive. The lights flickered like a language I no longer understood.

And in that silence, something clicked. I reached for my laptop, opened a new browser tab, and searched for cheap plane tickets.

Chapter 9

The airport bathroom wasn't glamorous, but it was as good a place as any for a transformation. I stood in front of the mirror, tugging at the oversized sweater I'd thrown on for the flight. The leggings and scuffed sneakers I'd worn for "comfort" weren't doing me any favours. This was supposed to be a moment, and I looked more like Adam Sandler, than a woman about to see her first crush after years apart. It felt like prepping for a high school reunion. I needed to bring it.

Unzipping my suitcase on the tiled floor earned me a disapproving glare from a woman juggling a toddler and a diaper bag. She didn't understand me, and honestly, I didn't understand her either. Our lives were different galaxies. For her, this was just an airport layover. For me, this was potentially life-changing.

This wasn't a casual reunion. I was stepping into a maybe. Maybe something beautiful. Maybe a beginning. I mean, if I was flying across the country for a man, I sure as hell wanted to feel good doing it.

The outfit I pulled out felt like armor: a fitted black racerback tank that showed I'd grown up—grown into myself, really. It revealed the muscle in my arms and back, and I'd earned every line of it. Over it, a pale denim jacket. Distressed black jeans that gave me a confident stride. And suede booties that said, "I've got my life together, thank you very much." I wanted to look effortless but striking. Like I hadn't tried hard... but somehow looked damn good.

As I changed in the cramped stall, my heart began to race, not just with nerves, but with something I hadn't let myself feel in years. Hope. And... Damn. I did look good. He had to notice me now.

Ever since James and I started talking again, old feelings had crept back in. That the messiness of that New Year's Eve at the cabin was just a detour on the road to something real. Something lasting. Maybe we weren't ready back then. But maybe now, now that we'd lived a little, hurt a little, figured out who we were, maybe this was the moment we'd been waiting for. No more distractions. No more school drama or games. We knew the feelings were mutual. But could we build something real from the versions of ourselves we'd become?

I stepped out of the stall and gave my reflection a final once-over. Loose waves framed my face, the tank tucked just right into my jeans. I looked like a woman ready to reclaim her story. My phone buzzed in my bag, jerking me out of the fantasy. I fished it out, expecting Kristen—probably updating me on Mischa or teasing me about "stepping into a rom-com."

Instead, it was Adam. What the hell...

Adam: Hey. So… I've been thinking. A lot.

I frowned, thumb hovering over the screen.

Adam: Maybe we should just do it. Get married. Why not, right?

I froze. My chest tightened.

His words landed with a weight they'd never had before. Was this his version of a Hail Mary? A desperate, last-minute attempt to hold on, knowing I was about to walk into something he couldn't control?

For a long moment, I just stared. Thought about what to write. What could I even say? That I was chasing a feeling I hadn't been able to let go of since I was eighteen? That I needed to see James, to know if the dream I'd carried all this time had any roots in reality? I slipped the phone back into my bag without replying.

Adam wasn't my future—at least, not the one I'd been dreaming about. As I walked out of the bathroom and into the terminal, a wave of anticipation swelled in my chest. This wasn't just nostalgia or a longing for closure. This was a possibility.

I wish Mischa were here. She'd calm me down with one look. But she wouldn't have liked the chaos of this airport anyway. She was probably curled up in a sunbeam at home, getting spoiled by Kristen. Lucky dog. The boarding announcement echoed over the speakers. I stepped forward. Ready to find out.

Ping. Another vibration. Another text. Please don't let it be another proposal. I glanced down.

James: I can't wait to see you. It's going to be hard to keep my hands off you at the airport. You've been warned.

I didn't have time to respond before the flight attendant's voice reminded everyone to switch to airplane mode. But a rush surged through me. Was it the plane lifting or the idea that I might be flying straight into the rest of my life? My heart skipped. Literally stopped, maybe. The flight was short, maybe 20 minutes, just enough time to calm down. When I noticed the view out the window - I felt as if I'd been there before. But I've never been to British Columbia before. And when they announced "Welcome, we've just arrived in Comox" I felt a feeling that wasn't so familiar. The feeling of…calmness.

I kept picturing it: that cinematic airport reunion, dropped bags and all, being lifted and spun into a sweeping kiss in front of strangers who'd clap or smile like extras in a feel-good movie. As soon as my feet hit the tarmac, something shifted inside me. It felt like home. I couldn't explain it, not exactly. But the air was cool and clean, brushing against my cheeks like a soft welcome. I inhaled deeply. Something in me settled.

Inside the airport, I scanned the waiting crowd for James, wondering how many other reunions were unfolding, awkward ones, tearful ones, long-awaited ones. My heart thudded against my ribs. Then I heard it. "Sam!"

There he was. Just as I remembered, tall, scruffy, light brown hair tucked beneath a cap. My nerves flared, fluttering through my chest. How would this go? Would he kiss me? Sweep me up? Hug me like he meant it?

He didn't kiss me. Instead, he gave me a hug. Quick. Polite. The kind you give a co-worker at the airport, not someone you've missed at 3 a.m. in texts. Not fireworks. Not even sparklers.

"You look great," he said with a smile that didn't quite reach his eyes. "You too." I tucked a loose strand of hair behind my ear, fidgeting with the strap of my bag. My laugh almost slipped out, nervous and forced. This isn't how I imagined us.

We walked toward the baggage carousel, the silence between us thick with things we weren't saying. I watched the way he moved, hands in his pockets, casual as ever but there was a tension in his shoulders I didn't remember. A stiffness. Maybe he was nervous, too.

"How was the flight?" he asked, finally. "Good. You know, the usual—tiny seats, screaming baby two rows back. But manageable." He chuckled softly, but it sounded more like habit than humour. "Yeah. Flying sucks."

We hovered in small talk. The surface-level stuff. I hated it. Where was the guy who sent that bold, teasing text? The one who'd made me believe in this moment? This reunion? Maybe I'd set the bar too high. His voice from before echoed in my head: "Ready for whatever."

The conveyor belt roared to life, and we both turned, watching as bags tumbled down the chute. The noise filled the space between us, mechanical and impersonal, like a soundtrack for everything we weren't saying. "Are you hungry?" he asked. "We could grab food before heading to my place. Still about a two hour's drive." "Sure," I said, trying to match his casual tone. "That sounds great. I could definitely eat."

My suitcase emerged, and I stepped forward, reaching for it, but he beat me to it, lifting it with ease. "Got it," he said, lighter now, as if trying to shift the mood. "Thanks," I murmured. I wanted to say more, to ask him if he was okay, if we were okay. But I stayed quiet.

As we made our way outside, I glanced at him again, searching his face for something—anything, to tell me this was still the guy I'd fallen for in messages and late-night phone calls. Nerves, I told myself. We just need time to find our rhythm again.

Still, a whisper rose from somewhere deep inside: What if this isn't what you thought it would be? He pulled into a restaurant overlooking the ocean, and something in me lifted. "This place is one of my favourites," he said. "Hope it's not too busy."

We walked in, and for a moment, I let myself imagine it—us at a window seat, sunset glowing over the water, clinking wine glasses, and laughing like we belonged here. But then the host appeared, clipboard in hand, and a too-cheerful, "Do you have a reservation?"

"Sorry, I forgot this place needs a reservation. I totally spaced on calling ahead. We can go somewhere else," he says, already turning back toward the car.

"Oh, that's okay. I'm sure we'll find something great," I reply, forcing a smile. But inside, I'm annoyed. He forgot? This is one of his favourite places. He knew I was coming. He told me how excited he was, how he couldn't wait to show me all the amazing things we'd do together. And now this? It's not like reservations are some secret restaurant hacks.

I follow him back to the car, trying to shake it off. Maybe I'm overthinking, something I do often. I tend to read too much into things, let tiny annoyances snowball into full-blown catastrophes in my head. But still... it stings. A guy who's spent weeks hyping up this trip doesn't just forget. Right? Have I set the expectation too high?

At dinner at a nearby chain restaurant, fish tacos and small talk, I feel more at ease. Maybe he was just nervous. I mean, who isn't? I remind myself not to let small disappointments ruin this trip or how I feel. I choose grace, for him, for me, for what this is right now. We engaged in small talk, sharing bits of laughter, and as time passed, I grew more curious about what the next five days together would bring. He picked up the bill and we drove back to his house. I looked out the window and noticed how perfectly the treelines lined up, how calm the water was—like the whole scene had been placed there on purpose. I'd never seen anything like it. I'd been so wrapped up in traffic lights, skyscrapers, and packed sidewalks that I didn't even realize life could look so different outside of everything I was used to. We didn't say much, but I didn't care. I was just happy to be there.

"I'll give you more of a tour in the next few days," he says as he cracks open a Red Bull in his kitchen. "But I figured we could just relax today. Let you unwind from travelling."

"That sounds great, thank you."

"Don't be shy. My house is yours while you're here."

"Thank you for that," I say, smiling, though my thoughts are spinning. Why does this feel so... plain? Shouldn't there be more sparks, more magic? I hesitate, then blurt out, "Does this feel weird to you? Seeing me after all this time?"

He pauses mid-sip, eyes flicking to mine. "Weird? I mean… yeah, I guess a little. But not in a bad way." He sets the can down and leans against the counter. "It's just… surreal, you know? I've thought about this moment a lot, but now that you're here, it's like" He runs a hand through his hair, the other still holding his hat.

"Like what?" I ask gently.

"Like I'm afraid I'll screw it up," he admits, looking down for a second before meeting my gaze again. "It's been a long time, Sam. I don't want to mess this up." I take a step closer, leaning slightly into his space. "James, you're not going to screw this up," I say quietly. "We're just two people catching up after a long time. No pressure, okay?"

His gaze softens, and for the first time since I landed, I see the James I'd been hoping for, the one who sent that playful text, who made me believe this could be the start of something incredible. "Okay," he says with a quiet smile. "No pressure."

But as we move through the living room. I still feel the weight of the unspoken. There's a history between us, a thousand unanswered questions, and a future we can't yet predict.

For now, I let it be. Maybe we'll get to all of that. Or maybe, for tonight, it's enough just to be here. We head toward his bedroom. His bedroom is exactly what I expected from a man living alone, functional, not intentional. The queen-sized bed dominates the small room, dressed in plain gray sheets and a thin blanket that looks more like an afterthought than a welcome.

Two flat pillows sit side by side, one slightly rumpled, like he'd only just remembered to fluff it before I arrived. The nightstand holds a half-empty water bottle, a few random coins, and a phone charger tangled at the edge.

The walls are mostly bare, except for a single poster of a band I don't recognize. A precarious pile of laundry, clean, I think, rests on a chair in the corner. Overhead, a yellowish light casts a cold glow, doing little to warm the room.

It's not a bad room. Just… sparse. Like he doesn't spend much time here. Like he doesn't care much about it. I miss my bed. I miss Mischa. I decide to get ready for bed, it's late and with the long day of travelling, I feel done.

That night, I lie on one side of the bed, stiff as a board, while James stretches out on the other. The bed creaks as he shifts, his hand brushing briefly against the blanket between us. The space between us feels like miles, thick with unspoken tension. We talk a little—nothing deep, just idle chatter about his job and the town—but the words fade quickly, leaving only his steady breathing and the faint hum of the baseboard heater kicking on.

I stare at the ceiling, my thoughts racing. This is fine. Normal, even. Two adults sharing a bed, no big deal. But my heart doesn't get the memo. It hammers in my chest every time he shifts, hyper-aware of his warmth just inches away and the subtle scent of his cologne lingering on the pillow. Is that Axe? I thought he might make a move, but he didn't.

The question loops in my mind, relentless. I thought he might make a move. Maybe he's trying to be respectful? I'm not sure if I'm relieved or disappointed by his restraint.

Eventually, his breathing evens out. He's asleep. I roll onto my side, trying to get comfortable on the overly firm mattress, pulling the thin blanket tighter around me. The sheets smell faintly of laundry detergent, clean, generic, impersonal. I close my eyes, willing myself to drift off, but sleep doesn't come. Instead, I lie there, replaying every text, every flirty comment, every expectation I'd stacked up in the weeks leading to this moment. I don't know what I expected. He said he wanted me.

The morning is slow, relaxed, filled with small talk and a quiet breakfast. I hate small talk. His kitchen mirrors the rest of the house, clean enough, but void of personality. A mismatched set of mugs, a jar of instant coffee, and a toaster with crumbs wedged permanently in the corners. No plants. No art. No softness or warmth. Just the essentials. It's as if no one's ever tried to make this place feel like home.

Maybe it's been a while since a woman added any colour to his life.

By late morning, we're in his truck, cruising around the town he now calls home. He points out the highlights: the bakery with the best cinnamon buns, the local pub where everyone unwinds after work, the park that hosts the annual summer fair.

"You probably wouldn't last five minutes living here," he says casually as we pass a row of quaint houses. I glanced at him, caught off guard. "Why would you think that?"

He shrugs, one hand on the wheel. "It's small. Quiet. You're a city girl. I just think it'd be hard for you to adjust." A beat. "The closest Starbucks is an hour away." I laugh, too quickly. But the comment sticks. What does that even mean? Is he teasing, or is there something underneath? I steal a glance at his profile, his jaw is tight, like he's holding something back. The words linger, unsettling me more than I want to admit.

As we pass a scenic view of the water, I force a smile and shift the conversation. "So, about these famous cinnamon buns, how early do we need to get there to beat the line?"

I like this town. It's quiet. Different. But nice. I'm used to bustling streets, big box stores, endless food options, and a population that doesn't fit in a high school gym. Could I make a life here, if it came to that? Could I trade everything in for something this simple?

After the tour of the town, we head back to his place for a quiet night in. He makes me pasta for dinner, lets me pick the movie and we cuddle on the couch. He falls asleep and I lay still, appreciating the silence.

On the third night, he invited me to his parents' house for dinner. I'd been expecting it, he mentioned they'd want to meet me before I came, and I was hopeful. I brought the perfect outfit: a floral midi dress, a soft cardigan, and neutral flats that struck a balance between stylish and approachable. I wanted to make a good impression. It mattered, especially after the strange rhythm of the last few days.

But the evening didn't start smoothly. "Sam! We need to leave in ten minutes. Are you ready?" James's voice cut through the house, sharp and impatient. I glanced at the clock, confused. "I thought we were leaving at six? It's only 5:40." He appeared in the doorway, keys in hand, his jaw clenched. "We don't have time for this. My mom hates when people are late. We're already cutting it close."

I opened my mouth to respond, but stopped myself. Instead, I rushed to finish my mascara, my hand trembling slightly. His tone stung, sharp as a slap. I'd been ready on time, but somehow, I still felt like I'd failed. He sighed, pacing the hallway, tension radiating off him. For a second, I thought he might actually honk the horn, like an impatient dad waiting in the driveway.

Finally, I grabbed my bag and slipped on my shoes, rushing to meet him at the front door. "Okay, I'm ready," I said, trying to keep my voice calm. "About time," he muttered, holding the door open. The frustration in his tone made my chest tighten.

The drive was silent, the kind of silence that presses on your chest. I stared out the window, watching trees blur into streaks of green and gray, wondering what kind of evening lay ahead. The air in the car was thick with unspoken thoughts. I sank deeper into the seat, unsure if I should say anything—or what I'd even say if I did.

When we pulled into the driveway of a modest but inviting house, I took a deep breath and braced myself. James turned off the ignition and glanced at me. "Just... try to relax, okay? My family can be a bit much sometimes." I forced a smile. "Don't worry, I'll be fine."

Inside, the house was warm and inviting, filled with the scent of baked ham and something sweet—maybe apple pie. Laughter drifted from the dining room, and the atmosphere was alive with voices. As we stepped in, James' mom appeared with a wide smile and open arms.

"You must be Samantha!" she exclaimed, wrapping me in a hug that was both genuine and a little overwhelming. "It's so nice to finally meet you. We've heard so much about you." "Thank you for having me," I said, returning the smile.

As we walked into the dining room, my heart dropped. This wasn't just a casual family dinner—it was a full-on celebration. Balloons floated in the corner, and a banner above the fireplace read: **Happy Birthday, Dad!**

I leaned closer to James, whispering, "Why didn't you tell me?" He shrugged, not meeting my eyes. "Didn't think it was a big deal." But it was. I felt blindsided, unprepared, and suddenly out of place.

The table was crowded with extended family, all laughing. I tried to stay afloat in the conversation, but the questions came fast and layered, how James and I met, what I did for work, whether I'd ever consider moving here. It was a lot.

Meanwhile, James slipped into the scene like he belonged there, cracking jokes, telling stories, completely at ease. I envied his comfort while I tried to mask how off-balance I felt, alone in the middle of a crowd.

Eventually, the dinner grew looser. The wine flowed, and though I tried to pace myself, James's mom kept refilling my glass. My nerves didn't help. Soon, I was buzzed, maybe more than buzzed. James was on his second—or third—beer when someone brought out a bottle of scotch. A toast was made, glasses clinked, and the room filled with laughter that felt both warm and dizzying.

By the time we stepped outside, the cool night air hit my skin like a relief. I wobbled slightly on the uneven path. James reached for my elbow, steadying me. "You're drunk," he teased, his grin soft and crooked. "And you're not?" I shot back, gesturing toward the flush creeping up his neck.

He chuckled, his hand sliding from my elbow to the small of my back. The touch was light, but it sparked something—warm, electric, and impossible to dismiss. We walked in silence, the only sounds the crunch of gravel beneath our feet and the whisper of leaves in the breeze.

Then, he stopped. I turned toward him, brows raised. "What?" His expression had shifted, less playful, rawer. "Sam," he said, voice low and slightly unsteady. "There's something I've been meaning to tell you."

My pulse quickened. I parted my lips to respond, but before I could speak, he stepped forward, hands slipping around my waist. His lips were on mine, warm, urgent, tasting of beer and something older, heavier. Regret. Longing. Years of what-ifs.

When he finally pulled back, he rested his chin against my forehead, breath coming fast. "I love you," he whispered, the words tumbling out like they'd been waiting fifteen years to be said. "I've always loved you."

I stared at him, my chest tight with a mix of emotions I couldn't quite name. Love. Relief. Confusion. It all swirled together, messy, electric, impossible to untangle. "James…" I whispered, unsure of what came next. But he didn't wait.

He kissed me again, deeper this time, his hands pulling me close, like he was afraid I might slip through his fingers. And in that moment, all the tension and uncertainty of the past few days cracked open into something reckless and consuming.

By the time we made it back to his place, we barely got through the front door before he was on me again. Our clothes hit the floor in a trail that led straight to his bedroom, like we were tumbling backward in time—back to that New Year's Eve so many years ago.

It was clumsy. His hands fumbled with my buttons. My knee knocked against the edge of the bed. We collapsed in a tangle of limbs and laughter. But it was us. Raw. Unfiltered. Imperfect. Afterward, tangled in the sheets, his arm draped over my waist with a kind of casual possessiveness, I stared at the ceiling and wondered: had anything really changed? Was I still the girl from fifteen years ago—still hoping to be chosen? And was he still the man who only wanted me when no one else was looking?

Over the next few days, he didn't repeat the words he'd said to me that night. He didn't confirm that he meant them. Instead, we spent our time drinking with his friends, playing it cool, as if nothing had been confessed in the dark.

But in those close moments, those in-between silences, I felt wanted. I felt like I was exactly where I was supposed to be. Then a message from Kristen lit up my phone.

Kristen: Hope you're having a great time. Just checking in, Mischa's doing great! I've been walking her every day and staying at your place until you're back. All is good here. But you do have to come back eventually... We miss you!

It was exactly what I needed. *Thanks, girl. I miss you both so much and can't wait to see you. Soooo much to talk about. See you soon!*

No, it wasn't the trip I'd dreamt of. It didn't go the way I imagined. But maybe I didn't even know what I was hoping for. So much history had been jammed into just a few days. Maybe we needed more time to understand what this was.

On the drive to the airport, he doesn't say a word. The silence is so loud I feel like I might break it just by breathing. "Thanks for everything," I finally say. "For letting me into your world... for letting me stay at your place... for interrupting your sp—"

He cuts me off with a laugh. "You didn't interrupt anything," he says. "Thank you for coming. I had a great time this week." My throat tightens. This is it. "About what you said the other night..." I pause. I can't believe I'm saying it out loud. "I love you too."

He grabs my hand and presses a kiss into it. A soft warmth spreads through my chest, relief, maybe. Or hope. A quiet confirmation of everything I'd been longing to believe. So, I let go of the doubt. I let go of all the uncertainties.

Chapter 10

It's been three months since I came back to reality. And it didn't take long, just hours after I landed, for the silence of my apartment and the buzz of the city to start feeling suffocating. Even though my trip to see James lasted only five days, leaving the city had exposed me to something I'd never felt before. A different kind of life.

Being with James in that small town, away from the chaos, made me realize I didn't want to just get through each day anymore. I wanted to live in them. Be present for the moments instead of watching them pass me by like scenery outside a window.

I remembered how my lungs felt fuller there. How the air didn't taste like exhaust and burnt espresso. I remembered how James made me laugh. How sometimes, when I caught him looking at me, it was like I was the only thing in the room that made any sense.

Since I left, James has called every day. Sometimes more than once. A quick check-in before he went to work, then again in the evening, asking how I was, telling me how much he missed me. He started sending photos of sunsets from his back deck. Always with a caption like ***Wish you were here, or this view would be better with you in it.***

He said he wanted me there. Maybe, this time, we could really make it work. And I wanted to believe him. But sometimes, his words and his actions didn't quite match.

One night, I woke to my phone buzzing again and again on the nightstand. It was nearly 3 a.m. James was calling, Face Timing, actually. I hesitated, still groggy, then answered. His face filled the screen, grinning wide. It didn't take long to realize he was drunk.

"Heyyyy," he slurred, chuckling like he was in on some private joke. "You look so cute and sleepy." "James? It's three in the morning. Are you okay?"

"Yeah, yeah, I'm good. I was out with some people from work. Just got home. This girl wanted me to go back to her place with her, but..." He leaned closer to the camera, his smile lopsided. "I came home instead. I wanted to see your face. Choose you, Sam. I chose you."

He looked so proud of himself, like he'd just passed some impossible test. My stomach twisted. "That's... good," I said quietly, unsure of what else to say. "You know what that means, right? I'm serious about you. I didn't go home with her. I came home for you." Eventually, he passed out mid-sentence. I hung up and stared at the screen, the glow still warm on my fingertips.

The next morning, the feeling still lingered—something sour in my gut I couldn't shake. On one hand, he had come home. He called me. He said the right things. But on the other hand... why was that even a decision he had to make?

Why did it feel like I was supposed to be grateful he didn't sleep with someone else? I told myself he was just drunk. People say dumb things when they drink. But the uneasiness followed me through the next few days like a shadow. Still, I kept moving.

Wake up. Drink coffee. Read. Walk Mischa. Work. Go to the gym. Play with Mischa. Sleep. Repeat. I deleted everyone's number from my phone. Even Adam's.

I hadn't heard from him since his proposal, and I wasn't expecting to. I didn't want to. My heart was with James now, even if he was across the country. Even if everything between us still felt unfinished. Maybe one day soon, we'd be together again.

This past year, I've poured myself into healing. I've been trying to understand how I even got here in the first place. Every third week, I show up for therapy—working through the divorce, peeling back the layers of anger I'd been too scared to touch for years. For the first time in a long time, I'm learning to let the feelings come, instead of always holding them in.

I finally had a fresh start with my finances, and for the first time in a long time, I could breathe. There wasn't a lot coming in, but it was enough—enough to pay rent, buy groceries, treat myself to Starbucks once a week, even meet friends for lunch or dinner. I could tuck a little aside for emergencies, maybe even for the future. After so much uncertainty, stress, and fear, it felt good to be on track. My life was beginning to take shape again. I was starting to feel… happy. Really happy.

The cold was creeping in again. Another harsh winter. And suddenly, I found myself wondering—why had I chosen to stay somewhere where being outside felt unbearable for half the year? Every conversation with James made me a little jealous of the West Coast weather. Sure, it still got chilly, and there was the occasional snowfall, but it wasn't this. It wasn't the kind of cold that made your face ache the moment you stepped outside.

Now that I had a glimpse into another kind of Canadian winter, I couldn't stop asking myself why I'd tolerated this one for so long. I didn't know it could be different. But now… the idea that life could be different felt like hope.

Maybe it could be my life—one where I could wake up, take Mischa out for a walk, and not feel like the air was punishing me for existing.

I was on my way to meet Kristen for lunch at our usual coffee shop. It had been months since I'd seen her, too long—and we had a lot to catch up on. She'd just returned from solo travelling across Europe, and we were both itching to swap stories, secrets, and everything in between. Every meet-up with her felt like therapy with a side of fries.

"There she is!" Kristen called, standing to wrap me in one of those hugs that reminds you exactly why you love someone. "I feel like I haven't seen you in, like, a hundred years," I said, sliding into the chair across from her. "You haven't! And I have so much to tell you. But first—spill everything. You look different. Glowy. Did you meet someone? Change up your skincare routine? Are you pregnant?"

Her eyes sparkled, and she leaned in dramatically like we were still teenagers gossiping by our lockers. I laughed. "Actually, no. None of those. But I did reconnect with someone." Her eyebrow arched. "Do tell." "Remember James from back in the day?" "You mean James, James? First-time-ever James?" "Yes. First-time-ever James."

I gave her the Cliff Notes version—James, the trip, how different it felt this time. I told her about the quiet little town, the kind of silence that calms your nervous system, the stars that actually felt visible. I told her how, for the first time in years, I felt like I could really breathe.

Then, I shared something I hadn't said out loud yet, craving some kind of validation—even just a raised eyebrow of encouragement. "I'm thinking about moving there." "What?" Her voice shot up in pitch. "No way. Are you serious?

Like, moving-moving? Across the country? Was the trip really that good?"

"It wasn't really about the trip," I said slowly. "It was more about how I felt while I was there." Kristen tilted her head and studied me, her expression softening with that intuitive insight she always had.

"You know what's funny?" she said. "I've seen you chase everything—jobs, relationships, apartments—but I don't think I've ever seen you chase peace. Maybe this is you finally doing that."

That's exactly what I felt. I didn't just want a change of scenery. I wanted a change of life. "Am I crazy for thinking about moving across the country for someone?" I asked. "Is it too fast? Impulsive? People are going to think I've lost it."

"Maybe they will. But who cares?" She shrugged. "You don't need anyone else to get it. If it feels right to you, that's enough. Honestly? You've already done 'safe.' Maybe it's time to see what happens when you don't play it safe."

She smiled; the kind that made you feel like you weren't as lost as you thought. "Why do you think I take those solo trips to places I've never been?" she added. "It's not always about where I go, it's who I become when I'm there."

We fell into conversation about her travels, what she'd seen, who she'd met, where she wanted to go next. I always felt so grounded after spending time with people who really saw me, who showed up without judgment and made space for my mess. It reminded me that I needed to let go of the judgment I sometimes held toward others. People make choices we don't always understand—but that's okay. It's their life, not ours. If it feels right for them at that moment, isn't that enough?

We said our goodbyes and went our separate ways. But I wasn't ready for the conversation to end. There was one more person whose advice I needed, my sister, Carrie. As soon as I got into my car, I dialed her number, hoping she'd be free for a quick chat on the drive home.

"Hey stranger," she answered on the second ring.

"Long time no chaos. What's up?"

I smiled. "You free to talk? I have something I want to run by you."

"Absolutely. Hit me."

"I'm thinking about moving to be with James."

There was a pause, not heavy with judgment, but careful, thoughtful. The kind of silence that says I'm listening.

"Ooohhh, I knew it!" she said finally, drawing out the words with delight. "I knew you'd come home all in love and want to pack up your life and hit the road."

I laughed. "How did you know that?"

"Because we're sisters. And if you remember, four years ago, that's exactly what I did."

She was right. One day, she just decided her life wasn't giving her what she needed. She packed up her car, drove to the East Coast to stay with a close friend, and ended up meeting her now-husband. The rest was history. I don't care for him but as long as she's happy.

I let out a long breath, surprised by how much I needed to hear that. "Yeah…" I said. "I guess I didn't think of it like that."

"It's scary," she continued. "People might call it impulsive or crazy, but when I left everything behind and moved, it wasn't for anyone else. It was about the life I wanted. And I could feel that life calling me, louder than anything else."

"Yes. That's exactly how I feel. Like there's this pull to a new life."

"No matter what you choose, someone will have unsolicited advice. If you stay, they'll say you're settling. If you go, they'll say you're reckless. So you might as well do what you want. Honestly, crazy sounds more fun, don't you think?" She was right. Still, one thought lingered, holding me back from bringing it up to James.

"But what if it doesn't work out, Care? What if I move, uproot my whole life, and it all crashes down?"

"Well, sure, there's a 50% chance that happens. But there's also a 50% chance it becomes the best decision you've ever made. Isn't that worth finding out?"

"Yeah... I guess it is. Thanks, Care. I needed to hear that."

"And if it doesn't work out," she said, voice warm and mischievous, "I'll fly over, help you pack, and we'll steal his phone chargers and remove the batteries from all his remotes."

"You're giving way too much 'partner in crime' energy right now... but not gonna lie, it's comforting. Also slightly alarming."

"I'm here for it."

"Thank you. Seriously. Just knowing you're in my corner means everything."

"You're welcome, sissy. It's your life. We're only here once—so go after what you want. And whatever happens, I've got you."

"Thank you. I'm home now—gonna take Mischa for a walk. I'll text you later."

"Okay, sounds good. Love you."

"Love you too."

We hung up. I stayed in the car for a moment, smiling to myself. A quiet, knowing laugh slipped out, a laugh that said this is right. The decision was unfolding naturally. All I had to do now was see if James was on the same page, and make it happen.

Inside, I kicked off my shoes and peeked down the hallway. Mischa lay sprawled across my bed. Her ears perked up when she saw me. "Hi, my baby," I cooed, stroking her head. "Wanna go for a walk?" She sprang up, shook herself off, and bolted to the front door. "I'll take that as a yes."

Our walks were like non-therapy therapy, quiet, grounding, restorative. I've done talk therapy plenty of times and love it, but something about walking a dog clears the noise. It centres me, gives space for the answers to rise up.

By the time we made it back, forty minutes later, I was ready. Ready to ask James the question that had been bubbling up all day. I sent him a message: *Hey, how's your day going? Do you have some time to FaceTime?* A few minutes later, he replied:

James: Hey babe, I'm just at my parents. Heading home in about 20, can I call you then?

Sure, no problem. Talk soon xoxx

Those 20 minutes felt like three hours. I was buzzing, anxious and excited. Was he as serious as I was? Would he understand what this meant for me?

Thirty minutes passed. Still no call. I cleaned the kitchen. Straightened a laundry pile I had zero intention of folding. Then I curled up on the couch beside Mischa and grabbed the book on the coffee table, ***The Friend Zone by Abby Jimenez.*** One of my current projects on a new release. It was peppered with sticky notes and colour-coded tabs. I'd been annotating it, figuring out how to make my own content more layered, more magnetic.

One hour later, my phone finally lit up. FaceTime Video from James, I slid my finger across the screen. He was outside on his back deck, bundled in a hoodie, a cigarette glowing between his fingers. He looked tired, his hair tousled, but he still gave me that half-smile that melted me every time.

James: "Hey, babe."

Exhaling a stream of smoke into the night.

"Sorry it took so long. You know how it is, trying to leave and getting stuck in the doorway while your mom tells you all the town gossip."

"I get it. It's okay. I'm just glad to see you now."

James: "So, what's up? How was your day?"

"It was really good, actually. I wanted to talk to you about something." I hesitated for a beat. The words were there, sitting right on the edge of my tongue, but suddenly they felt massive, like saying them out loud would crack something open I wasn't sure I could close. "Well," I said slowly, "I had a really good visit with you. And I miss you."

James: "I miss you too."

A pause stretched between us.

"I was just thinking…" I trailed off, then pushed through the lump in my throat. "Maybe we shouldn't wait so long for the next one? "

James leaned back in his chair, exhaling before speaking.

James: "What do you mean?"

"Like... maybe we don't do the long-distance thing anymore."

He blinked, caught off guard.

James: "You're thinking of planning another trip soon?"

He leaned forward then, eyes narrowing like he was making sure he'd heard me right.

James: "Wait—are you serious? The cigarette paused halfway to his lips."

I nodded slowly, offering a half-smile, trying to soften the weight of what I was about to say. "I mean, yeah. I've been thinking about it a lot. Since I got back, nothing here feels the same. It's too loud, too fast. But there? With you? I felt... peaceful. Like it made sense. You make sense."

He sat back again, took a long drag from the cigarette, and exhaled with a quiet sigh.

The screen shook a little as he adjusted his phone. I could hear the familiar creak of his patio chair underneath him.

James: "That's a pretty big move, Sam."

"I know," I said quickly. "I know it's fast. But we already know each other. Things felt so natural between us. I'm not saying I'll show up tomorrow with my boxes taped shut, but... I want to know if this is something you could see too. If we're on the same page."

He scratched the back of his neck, gave a small laugh like he was still catching up to the conversation.

James: "I mean... damn. Yeah. That's... wow."

Another pause. "I just didn't expect you to say that tonight."

"I didn't expect to feel this way either," I admitted. "But I do." He looked at me, really looked. And for a moment, I saw that version of James I'd fallen for on that first trip. The one who sent me pictures of sunsets and said he wished I was there.

James: "I think it could be really good. If we're careful, if we talk about expectations and stuff... yeah. I think we could make this work."

My heart fluttered. "Yeah?"

James: "Yeah. Let's talk about it more this week. Figure out a timeline, what it would look like. I'm not against it, Sam. Not at all. It's just... a lot. I want to do it right."

That last sentence hung in the air between us, gentle, grounding.

I smiled and nodded. "That's fair. I want that too." We stayed on the call a little longer, talking about logistics, money, how it might all play out. But underneath the planning, underneath the jokes and soft smiles, I felt something I couldn't quite name.

Not doubt, exactly. More like... a shift. A quiet rumbling in the foundation. It felt more like ticking off a checklist than making a leap together. Maybe that was the smart thing, to iron out the details, be realistic. Maybe love at this stage of life was supposed to be practical. Still, the idea of a new life in a new place, with someone familiar, felt safe. And safety had started to feel like its own kind of love.

The morning sun spilled in through the bedroom window, warm on my skin. Mischa was curled up at the foot of the bed, snoring softly, one paw twitching like she was mid-dream, chasing something.

I reached for my phone out of habit, half-expecting nothing, half-hoping for everything. A text from James lit up the screen.

James: Hey you. I've been thinking about our call last night. Can we talk soon?

My stomach flipped in that familiar, excited-nervous way it always did with him.

Of course. Just waking up. Call whenever you're free. Five minutes later, my phone lit up with his name. A regular call this time. I answered quickly, trying to keep my voice steady.

"Hey."

"Hey," he said. His voice was soft, clearer than last night. Like he'd been sitting with it, turning the idea over in his hands.

"You got a second?"

"Always," I said, crossing my legs under the covers.

"I didn't sleep much," he admitted with a small laugh. "Keep thinking about what you said. About moving."

My heart thudded in my chest. "Yeah?"

"Yeah. And... I think we should do it. I want you here, Sam. I want this. Us."

For a second, I forgot how to breathe. Joy, relief, disbelief, all of it rushed in at once, crashing together like a wave I didn't see coming. "You do?" I whispered.

"I do," he said. "I know it's fast, but it feels right. I spent most of the morning looking at the calendar, trying to figure out when it would make the most sense."

I pulled the blanket tighter around me, letting the moment settle in my chest. "Okay… when were you thinking?"

"I could fly out in about a month. That gives you time to wrap things up, your lease, and work. Then we could do the drive together. Make a trip out of it. You, me, Mischa. Just us."

I smiled, and this time it wasn't cautious or uncertain. It was real, full. "That actually sounds… amazing."

He laughed softly, a teasing warmth in his voice. "You sure you're ready for this kind of adventure with me?"

"I think I've been ready," I said, my voice quieter now. "I just needed to know you were too."

There was a pause, not awkward, not strained. Just a shared stillness. Like we'd both felt something shift, something unspoken settle into place.

"I'll book the flight tonight," he said.

"Okay," I murmured. A breath, barely audible. "This is really happening, huh?"

"It is," he said. "We're doing this."

When the call ended, I didn't move right away. I stared at the screen, blinking into the silence. The room felt both full and weightless. Mischa padded across the bed, her tiny paws pressing into the blanket, and climbed into my lap. She nestled against my chest, resting her head there like she could feel the storm inside me and was anchoring me through it.

I wrapped my arms around her, pressing my face into her fur.

A month.

I had one month to pack up my life. To say goodbye to the streets I could walk blindfolded, to my friends who have been close by for comfort, to the noise I used to mistake for comfort, to the version of me who had once felt rooted here.

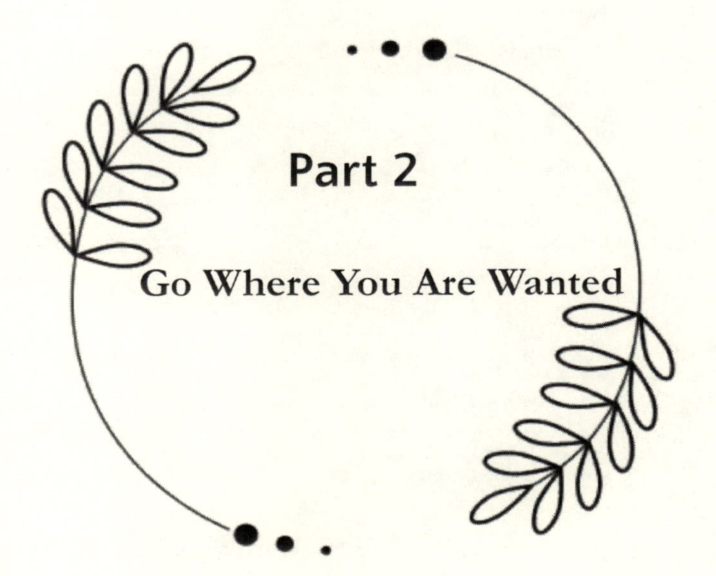

Part 2

Go Where You Are Wanted

Chapter 11

It didn't take long to pack up the life I was leaving behind. I fit everything I cared about into my car: the essentials, the sentimental, and the non-negotiable. I kept what mattered most and let go of the rest, donating, tossing, releasing pieces of a life that no longer fit. In the end, it all came down to books, some clothes, my computer, and of course, Mischa. The backseat was full—boxes stacked neatly to leave just enough space for Mischa to stretch out and for James's bag to squeeze in beside her.

I said goodbye to my friends, my apartment, and the version of life I once thought I wanted. Then I drove north, 12 hours, to where my parents lived and where James would land. It felt like closing a door and opening another, all in the same breath.

Of course I was nervous. Who wouldn't be? I was scared to fit in, scared of the change. Was I really ready to live with someone again? To start over? There was grief in the leaving, yes, but also hope. Hope for something better. Hope for shared mornings and lazy Sunday coffee. I was excited, too, excited for my family and friends to visit, excited to build something new with James. Something of ours.

He was flying in that late-afternoon, and we had two days before we'd head out together. Since he had old friends in town, it made sense to stay there before starting the journey.

I loved that he'd taken time off work to make the trip with me. It felt like he wanted this, wanted me. Like he was welcoming me into his world, not just tolerating the idea of it.

When I picked him up at the airport, he greeted me with a wide, warm smile and pulled me into a hug that swallowed me whole. I melted into him. In that moment, everything felt right. Seeing him again, holding him, it grounded me. I couldn't wait for him to meet my parents, my close friends. I wanted them to see how happy I was, how real this was becoming.

After we left the airport, I dropped him off at one of his friend's houses, someone he hadn't seen in years. I didn't mind that we were parting for a few hours. I had errands to run and friends to catch up with, and soon we'd have days together on the road. Long hours in the car, side by side. Just us.

For our road trip, I made sure we were fully stocked. His favourite energy drinks, his favourite songs played on the playlist I'd made, and his favourite snacks sat within arm's reach. I wanted him to feel how much I appreciated him coming with me. The trip would likely take up to five long days, maybe more if we took our time. James had taken two weeks off work, so there was no real rush to get back. I wanted to experience this road trip, not just survive it.

I had it mapped out in my mind, stopping for a night in Banff, seeing Lake Louise, winding slowly through the Rockies. We'd probably hit snow, so I built in a buffer day in case we needed to stop. I wanted it to be beautiful. Memorable. Ours.

There's something raw and revealing about a road trip. When you're stuck in a car with someone for hours, all the small talk fades, and real conversations surface. Layers peel back. You get to know the silences as much as the words. I was looking forward to getting to know him again.

Travelling with Mischa was always easy. She'd peek up at first, curious where we were going this time, then curl up in the back and sleep through most of it. She'd done so many trips before that I didn't even consider the possibility this one might affect her differently. This was also the first time she'd meet James. She loved everyone I brought around her. Everyone.

So, it surprised me, startled me, actually, when we got back to the hotel that first night and she didn't greet him. She didn't even come close. She curled up on the opposite side of the room, as far away from us as she could.

The day before we left, I brought James to meet my parents. It felt like a kind of ceremony, having them send us off. My dad, of course, couldn't resist giving us a checklist: drive safe, take your time, see this, skip that, eat here. James reassured him with confidence, promising he'd keep me and Mischa safe, that we'd soak in the journey and stay ahead of the weather.

My parents really liked him. My dad even said he was happy for me, that he couldn't wait to visit once we were settled. James offered for them to stay with us, said he'd love to show them around. Everything felt like it was clicking into place.

So, I said goodbye to everything I knew, my family, my city, my routine, and packed it all up for a new life with James on Vancouver Island. It was surreal how fast it happened. Six months ago, I'd only just visited. Now, I was moving.

James wanted us to leave by 5 a.m., so we packed the car the night before, made space for Mischa, and tried to get a good night's sleep. It was strange lying there, realizing that with one decision, my whole life had changed. Still, Mischa hadn't warmed up to James. Anytime he reached to pet her, she'd just stare at him, then move further away. I'd never seen her act that way before.

I had envisioned the road trip as a chance to reconnect, just us, laughing, exploring, sharing old playlists and new memories. I thought Mischa would grow comfortable with him. That it would be good. But on that first leg of the trip, I think I realized... it wasn't going to be any of those things.

I drove the first six hours. The weather was clear, the roads dry, and the sky stretched out in that soft, bright blue only road trips can offer. It was peaceful. When we pulled off for our first stop, to swap drivers, let Mischa out, and grab some food, I felt a shift. It was subtle. A ripple under the surface. But something in the air changed.

For the past three months, I'd been fairly strict with Keto. I felt good, energized, clear, and it had become second nature. So, when I ordered a burger without the bun, wrapped in lettuce, I didn't think twice.

But James made me feel small. Right there in front of the cashier, he scoffed. "Nobody knows what you're talking about. Order off the menu."

His tone was sharp. Belittling. I tried to laugh it off. "James, this is how I eat now. I just haven't eaten bread lately." "Sam, don't be an idiot. Order it properly." The cashier looked uncomfortable. So, did I. I turned to the guy at the counter, my voice quiet but steady. "Is that something you can do? Just lettuce wrap it?" He nodded. "Yeah, no problem. Same price, though."

"That's fine. Thank you." I turned to James. "See? All good." James didn't reply. He placed his order next, his voice pointed. "I want my burger like a normal person. With the bun." He didn't even look at me.

I didn't say anything, but I felt small.

We grabbed our burgers to go and hit the road again—James behind the wheel this time. Mischa hovered over me the entire ride. When I finished eating, she climbed from the backseat onto my lap and stayed there until we stopped for the night.

I booked a hotel in Saskatchewan so we could rest and get an early start the next morning. I'd hoped we could sleep in, take it slow. But James was firm—we had to leave by 5 a.m.

The first night wasn't what I expected. Even though we were together, physically close, it felt like miles stretched between us. We barely spoke. I didn't know what I'd done or why the air between us suddenly felt so cold.

By 5 a.m., we were back on the road—just like he wanted. We made a quick stop for coffee, and James slid into the driver's seat as we left another province behind.

Instead of sitting in the thick silence, I broke it.

"Thank you for doing this road trip with me," I said gently, resting my hand on his thigh. "It really means a lot to have you here."

I wanted to start fresh. Reset from whatever went wrong yesterday.

"Yeah?" he said, his tone edged with sarcasm. "You've got a funny way of showing it, Sam. Why didn't you tell me you eat like that?"

The comment hit sideways. I blinked, pulling my hand away.

"Eat like what?"

"Like a rabbit. How are we supposed to live together and make meals if I don't eat that way?"

I stared at him, trying to piece together the logic. The words didn't make sense—not really. People in the same household ate differently all the time. When I lived with Josh, he was trying to bulk up while I was counting macros and losing weight with a trainer. Our meals were totally different, but it worked. It was never an issue.

"James, I don't think it's that big of a deal," I said carefully. "We don't have to eat the same way."

He shook his head, eyes fixed on the road. "How am I supposed to know what you can eat or how to cook for you?"

I paused, measured my words. "Well... you could always ask. Try to understand why I eat the way I do." Silence. Long, uncomfortable, thick silence. Still nothing from him.

The highway vanished in front of us, swallowed by a growing snowstorm. The world outside turned white—blinding and endless. James kept his eyes on the road. I stayed quiet, afraid to push any further, especially in weather like this. I let it go. Focused on what was ahead.

Suddenly, the car's Bluetooth came to life—my phone ringing through the speakers, cutting through the silence and startling both of us.

It's my dad.

I pick up. "Hi, Dad."

"Hey, just checking in. How are you two doing? Where are you now?"

"We're good. Just driving into Alberta, but we've hit the start of a really bad snowstorm."

"Yeah, I figured. The weather network's been showing some nasty stuff. It doesn't look like it's letting up anytime soon. You might want to think about stopping somewhere for the night, finding a hotel, and riding it out."

That was my dad—his way of keeping me safe, even from miles away. "Yeah, that's probably a good idea. We can barely see anything."

"Okay. I won't keep you—drive safe, both of you. And call me if you need anything, okay?"

"Thanks, Dad. Love you."

"Love you too."

When I hung up, James didn't say a word. He just kept driving, both hands on the wheel. I didn't say anything either. I was scared. The snow thickened with every passing kilometre, white swallowing the road. We slowed down, but the highway was still slick and unpredictable. The silence between us pressed in like the frost on the windshield.

We chain-smoked as we drove. Neither of us said it aloud, but the nerves were obvious. Since getting back from my trip, I've started having the occasional cigarette and I'm not regretting the pack I bought for this trip.

When we eventually stopped for gas and more snacks, James looked at me and asked, "Can you take the wheel for a few hours? I'm getting tired." I hesitated. He'd been carrying the weight of navigating through the storm, and I didn't want to add more pressure. I nodded. "Yeah, I can drive."

My stomach was a knot, but I'd handled harsh Ontario winters before. I could do this. Secretly, I'd hoped we could spend the night in Banff. I'd already picked out a charming hotel I was willing to splurge on. A cozy night. A warm bath. A break from the tension. It sounded like exactly what we needed.

"Did you want to stay in Banff tonight?" I asked, trying to sound light. "Maybe we could take a walk and enjoy the scenery?"

James didn't even look at me. "Absolutely not. We need to keep driving."

"But… we're not in a rush. Maybe we could just take a break, slow down a bit."

"Sam, we're not stopping in Banff. We'll find a motel in a couple hours. Drop it." That was the end of that.

Later, on the Coquihalla Highway, I kept my speed around 90 km/h. The road dipped and twisted in steep descents, snow swirling in the headlights. My palms were sweating. Not just from the road—but from him. James sat beside me, watching every move. Tension coiled tight.

When I braked gently on the descent, he snapped. "Why the hell are you driving so slow? We're not going to die because you're too scared to drive downhill." I said nothing, too focused on the icy road, too full of dread to answer. But inside, I was shaking.

Mischa stirred in the backseat, restless. Her little head poked out, ears perked. Even she could sense the shift in the air. Just get us off this highway. Just get to the bottom, I told myself. When we finally did, I pulled into a rest stop, slammed the gear into park, and climbed out.

"Drive," I snapped, tossing him the keys. "I'm done." James scowled. "Wow, Sam. No reason to be such a bitch about it." I glared at him, fury and fear swirling in my chest. "You yelled at me the entire time. What did you expect? That's not how you help someone get through a snowy highway when they're already scared."

Mischa leapt from the backseat into my lap the moment I sat down. She was trembling.

We made it to Kelowna for the night and found a rundown motel. I didn't speak for the rest of the drive. I had nothing left to say. I felt invisible. Like I didn't matter. Maybe the pressure of this trip was too much for us. Maybe we were already unraveling.

Chapter 12

It's been a month since the move, and I was starting to believe, maybe, I could make this work. The road trip left its mark on Mischa. She flinched when James's voice rose too loud, or disappeared under the table the moment he stepped through the door. That wasn't like her. Mischa had always been warm, affectionate, the kind of dog who nestled into you like she belonged there. But with James, it was different. Like she didn't know who she was allowed to be.

Some mornings, I'd wake to find a puddle in the hallway, or worse. At first, I told myself she just needed time to adjust. New surroundings, new routine, new people. But a small voice inside wondered if she was trying to tell me something. Dogs can do that, right? Pick up on things we bury deep, things we don't want to name yet.

She always knew when I felt safe. When I was grounded around people, she'd relax too. But lately, she'd been on edge, and maybe it was because I was. I wanted to believe this unsettled feeling was just part of the transition. That it was normal to feel uncomfortable.

To feel fragile.

Trying to settle into an unfamiliar house with someone you have history with feels like rewriting a book you never finished.

The plot twists don't land. The characters feel off. And the more I tried to reconcile who James used to be with who he was now, or who I wanted him to be, the more it all felt... hollow.

For the first time since we arrived, I unpacked a box that wasn't a priority. Just some books and little knick-knacks, things meant to make a space feel more like mine. Four boxes remained untouched, stacked in the closet like silent sentinels.

Something about them felt final. Like opening them would mean I was really here. That I had chosen *this*.

Chapter 13

Spring was beautiful, different from back home. There was something cleaner in the air, something alive. The days carried a warmth that felt like possibility, and if you paid close enough attention, you could almost feel the seasons shifting.

James worked long hours, sometimes 12-hour shifts—which left me with plenty of time alone with Mischa. I threw myself into content creation for my book review channel, chasing brand partnerships, and searching for freelance gigs that might help chip away at the financial dent the move had made.

But no matter how busy I kept, the days melted into one another, a quiet loop of loneliness. Groundhog Day, but lonelier.

I even considered getting a job as a waitress. Not because I wanted to, but because the idea of a steady paycheck, and maybe even meeting new people, sounded like something solid to hold onto. There weren't many options nearby, but I often drove past a beachside resort about forty-five minutes away. Every time I passed it, I wondered what it would be like to be one of the smiling guests, someone who flew across the world to stay there.

One day, I told myself. One day, I'll stop and walk through the front doors like I belong. When James came home each evening, it was as if the air itself changed. I'd pause, listening for the creak of the door, the shuffle of his boots, trying to read his mood before I said too much. Some nights, rare, golden ones, he'd be warm. He'd smile. He'd ask about my day.

But more often, I braced myself. It felt too familiar. Like walking on eggshells in my childhood home. Before I moved in, James used to text me constantly. Even during work. He'd ask what I was up to, send me updates about his day, crack jokes, flirt with me. But after I moved in?

Radio silence until he got home, and even then, his mood was unpredictable. Cranky. Short. Irritable. Some days, he'd barely speak. Other days, I'd get the cold shoulder for reasons I didn't understand.

And yet… there were nights he'd come through the door beaming, greet Mischa with belly rubs, offer to help with dinner, pick a movie, clean the dishes afterward. I started to wonder if this was just what living with someone was like. I didn't have much to compare it to.

I'd only lived with one other person before, and I don't remember Josh ever being like this. Sure, he had a temper, but it was never directed at me or Mischa. His anger had targets like video games or kitchen appliances. Like the time the oven stopped working right as he was halfway through cooking Thanksgiving dinner.

James's behaviour felt different. More personal. It reminded me of my mom. She had a short fuse, too. I used to monitor her every expression, every breath, tiptoeing through my childhood just trying not to set her off. Was this the same thing, replaying itself with a different face?

Some days, James would come home and kiss me. He'd ask about my day, suggest dinner out or a trip to the next town. We'd curl up on the couch, pick a show to binge, and for a while, those nights felt like what I thought adult love might be. Respectful. Safe. Real. On those days, my anxiety felt like a stranger. But it never stayed that way for long. Because before I knew it, my nervous system would start buzzing, my body reminding me that safety was temporary. That the other version of him might walk through that door next time. That's when I had my first panic attack.

It happened not long after I moved in, when he lost it because I hadn't changed my phone number to the local area code. The fight that followed... It felt like a hurricane I didn't see coming. I didn't understand why it mattered so much. That seemed to enrage him more. He didn't just want me to comply, he wanted me to get it.

The delay in changing my car registration and licence only made things worse. But the truth was, I simply didn't have the extra money to make those changes. I was scraping by. That didn't matter to him. Not understanding why it mattered to him made me feel small, confused, and like I was doing everything wrong again.

The stove clock read 6:30 PM. James would be home any minute. The scent of garlic and onions blanketed the kitchen, warm and inviting, as I smoothed a layer of ricotta and mozzarella over fresh pasta sheets. A separate baking dish—zucchini slices neatly stacked—sat beside it. My quiet protest against carbs.

The lasagna wasn't quite ready for the oven, but I was on track. I wanted tonight to feel a little special—a small gesture to show I cared, that I was still trying. That I was still his.

I hesitated, unsure if he'd want to eat right away or take time to decompress. In the end, I trusted my gut: I'd wait until he walked in, gauge his mood, and slide the dish in then. It wouldn't take long to bake.

Mischa lay sprawled at my feet, ears flicking at each sound from outside. She always sensed when James was close—some internal clock or instinct that I envied.

Right on cue, I heard the low rumble of his truck in the driveway, then the familiar slam of the door. A beat later, the front door swung open, and James stomped inside, each boot step landing like a warning. Mischa lifted her head but didn't move—her body tense, alert.

"Unbelievable," he muttered, dropping his bag by the door without a glance in my direction. "Just absolutely unbelievable." "Hey," I said softly, drying my hands on a dish towel. "Rough day?"

"Rough doesn't even begin to cover it," he snapped, yanking open the fridge and grabbing an energy drink. The can hissed as he cracked it. "Do you have any idea how useless people can be?" I stayed quiet, sensing the storm before it hit. I turned back to the lasagna, smoothing the final layer of cheese. I'd been hoping for a kiss hello—but those were rare these days.

"Marie screwed me over. Again." He began pacing the kitchen like a man trying to outrun his own rage. "I told her I needed the inspection report finalized this morning. You know what she sent instead? An email. With some half-assed excuse about running out of time. Now guess who's stuck with the fallout?"

I glanced up, unsure what to say. Marie. The ex. He'd mentioned her before—an ex-girlfriend turned colleague. The thought of her always made my stomach knot, though I tried not to let it show. I didn't know much, only what James had told me that they'd lived together for years, and then one day, she left.

"That's frustrating," I said carefully, hoping to soften his momentum before it turned into a full-blown rant. "Frustrating?" His laugh was bitter. "She's a mess. She always has been. Everything's about her. She doesn't think twice about how her screw ups affect other people."

I bit the inside of my cheek, the questions forming but never spoken. If she was so unreliable, why work with her? Why date her for so long? Why talk about her like she still lived under his skin? I focused on covering the lasagna with foil, the scent of tomato and garlic thick in the air. "I'm sorry you're dealing with that," I murmured.

"You don't get it, Samantha," he snapped, waving the can like a weapon. "You don't know what it's like to constantly have people dragging your work down. Making you look incompetent."

The words landed hard. Sharper than they needed to be. Still, I kept my voice even. "I wasn't trying to downplay it," I said. "I just—" "Is dinner ready yet?" he cut in, already turning away. "I'm starving." "Almost," I replied, slipping the lasagna into the oven. "It just needs about 30 minutes."

"Thirty minutes?" he echoed, incredulous. "You've been home all day, and you didn't think to have it ready by now? I come home starving, Samantha. I don't want to wait all night for a damn meal."

Mischa shifted on the floor, her eyes flicking between us like she could sense the tension crackling through the air. I bent to give her a quick pat, her warm fur grounding me in a way nothing else could. "I wanted it to be fresh for you," I said quietly, trying to keep the peace. "Yeah, well, next time, start earlier," he snapped, slamming his can onto the counter. "You know I hate waiting."

Without another word, he stormed into the living room. Moments later, the blare of the TV filled the silence he'd left behind, sports highlights booming through the house like a second wave of noise meant to drown me out. "Sam?" he called over the TV. I poked my head around the corner, offering a half-smile. "Yeah?"

"Don't forget to transfer me your half of the grocery money." "Oh… okay." I hesitated. There was something strange about it, this tit-for-tat in a relationship. You owe me for this, you owe me for that. But that was James. And I said nothing.

I said nothing when he thought it was fair that I pay half for his case of energy drinks and three bags of liquorice, stuff I didn't touch. I said nothing to keep the peace. Again. I pulled out my phone and sent the transfer.

Back in the kitchen, I chopped vegetables for a salad. The rhythmic thunk of the knife against the cutting board steadied me, a small anchor in a house that no longer felt like mine. Mischa pressed into my leg, vibrating with quiet anxiety. Her presence reminded me I wasn't entirely alone. Not yet.

After dinner, I did the dishes while James disappeared into the basement to do whatever it was he did down there. Somewhere in the other room, my phone buzzed, a text. Kristen, maybe. Checking in.

Jackson. His name lit up the screen like a pulse.

I hadn't heard from him since the day I dropped him off and told myself that was it. No more looking back. But now, staring at his name, curiosity curled in my stomach like smoke. I clicked the message.

I miss your eyes.

My heart drops into my stomach. My throat tightens, eyes stinging with the start of tears. Did I give up too soon? I wonder what life might've looked like if I'd stayed. I can't. I deleted the message. The past doesn't belong in the present—not tonight. Not anymore.

I grab Mischa's leash. "Come on, girl. Let's take a walk." Just twenty minutes. Just enough time to breathe.

The air outside is crisp and laced with the scent of budding flowers and faint woodsmoke. Mischa trots ahead, tail wagging, ears perked. Her presence is grounding. For the first time that evening, I feel the tightness in my chest begin to ease.

Just a short walk. Just a small escape. I don't know why I go silent when he gets like that. It's like something inside me shuts down. I freeze—afraid that if I say the wrong thing, I'll make it worse. Careful not to make noise. Careful not to breathe wrong. It didn't feel like eggshells anymore, no, now it feels like shards of glass.

But this time... I'm choosing to walk through them instead of standing in them. I've been trying not to live in the past, yet, here I am, trying to create my future with memories. When I return, I unhook Mischa's leash at the door. Something feels off. The kitchen light is on. James is standing by the counter, arms crossed, jaw clenched. "Where were you?" His voice is sharp.

I blink, surprised by his tone.

"I just took Mischa for a quick walk. Around the block." My voice is steady, but soft.

"You didn't tell me," he says, voice rising. "You just disappeared. I didn't know where you were."

Mischa presses against my leg, picking up on the tension.

"James, I was gone for fifteen minutes. I had my phone."

"Yeah, well, you didn't answer it."

I frown and pull my phone from my pocket. No missed calls. No texts. "You didn't call or text me."

"That's not the point," he snaps, running a hand through his hair. "What if something had happened to you? I wouldn't even know where to look. Do you know how irresponsible that is?" I stare at him, feeling the ache return to my chest.

"I was just walking Mischa," I say, voice quieter now. "I didn't think I needed to announce every time I stepped outside."

"Well, maybe you should have," he shot back, eyes narrowing. "I was worried, Samantha. You could've been mugged, hit by a car, God knows what else. And I'm just supposed to sit here, not knowing where you are?"

His words hit harder than I expected—not because of what he said, but how he said it. Like I was a child who'd broken curfew. The heat of his concern masked a deeper accusation. Still, if he'd been so worried, why hadn't he just called?

I said nothing. I just wanted this conversation to end. I wanted to go to bed. "I appreciate that you were worried," I replied, my voice flat. "Next time, I'll let you know when I take Mischa out."

He scoffed, turning away for a moment before whipping back around. "I'm just trying to make you understand how inconsiderate it was to leave without saying anything." A knot tightened in my stomach, a tangle of guilt, frustration, and something deeper I couldn't name.

"I needed some air," I said quietly. "That's all. I didn't think I needed permission to walk my dog."

"It's not about permission, Samantha." His voice rose, sharp and strained. "It's about communication. It's about respect. Something you clearly don't understand."

Am I missing something? The question burned in my chest. I wanted to scream. What did I even do wrong? My heart raced. My throat closed. I couldn't speak. I turned away before the tears could win, motioning for Mischa to follow. We retreated to the bedroom, silent and sore.

I climbed under the covers and patted the bed. Mischa jumped up, circling once before settling on top of me, resting her head just beneath my chin. She wasn't usually a cuddler, not unless she was scared. That night, she didn't move. Neither of us did. It was like she was shielding me.

James never came to bed.

When I woke up the next morning, I found him sleeping on the couch.

Chapter 14

I stood at the counter, rinsing dishes after breakfast, my usual go-to: a bacon and cheese omelet, delicious and Keto-approved, the same routine I'd followed since just before I moved here. James came up behind me, wrapping his arms around my waist.

"A few of my coworkers are getting drinks on Saturday. Want to come with me?" he asked, his voice low and easy. It was the first time he'd ever invited me to meet anyone from work. And it felt like a milestone I wasn't sure I was ready for.

James rarely mentioned his colleagues, except for Marie and Lisa. Marie was "the ex." Lisa was "the one who got away." Once, he'd even called her "the one I wanted for a long time, but nothing ever happened." I still didn't know why he felt the need to tell me those things. Was he trying to be honest? Or was it just a power move?

Maybe this invitation was his way of closing the distance between us. Or maybe it was a test—to see how well I'd fit in, or if I'd even bother to go. "Oh… um, sure. Yeah, that sounds fun," I said. The words felt like a costume. Truth was, I didn't want to go. But I felt like I should. I needed to see the world he lived in when I wasn't around, the people he spent his hours with.

Things still felt weird between us after the lasagna fight. After he yelled at me for not telling him I was out walking Mischa. It was like he wanted to pretend it never happened. But since then, he'd been more attentive. Overly affectionate, even. Like he was trying to rewrite something.

"Great! So, what do you have going on today?" "Oh, I'm taking Mischa for a walk, then heading to the gym. After that, I'll work on some content for an upcoming review I'm putting together."

"Sounds like a good day," he said, his lips brushing against my neck, his grip tightening just enough to make me pause. "Maybe we can make it even better." His voice dipped, playful now, as his hands slid beneath the hem of my shirt.

"James..." I breathed, but he silenced me with a kiss. I kissed him back, hesitantly at first, my mind racing. This is what I wanted, right? For him to want me, to make me feel like I mattered. His hands moved with growing insistence, and for a moment, I let myself disappear into it. It felt good to be wanted, even if something about it felt wrong.

Afterward, I pulled on leggings and a hoodie, clipped Mischa's leash, and called out to James that I was heading out.

I needed air. Space. Time to clear my head. What just happened? Why did it feel so off, so hollow, being close to my own boyfriend?

We were barely intimate, not even close to what I expected. Before I moved here, he went on and on about how he wanted me all the time. About how he couldn't wait for us to live together and do it all the time. But now? Once a month, if that. And only when he initiated it.

I used to try. A lot. But after being turned down so often, I stopped. Rejection chips away at you after a while. Makes you shrink. Makes you question your desirability. And anyway, how could I want to be close when I was always bracing for the next mood swing? Waiting for the other shoe to drop. Honestly though, while he was rejecting the idea of me, my body was slowly rejecting him. My body couldn't relax around him.

I shoved in my earbuds, cranked the volume, and hit play on a Godsmack song. Mischa looked up at me, tail wagging, ready. "Let's go," I whispered. We ran.

After my run with Mischa and a solid workout at the gym, I jumped into the shower. As the hot water streamed down and I massaged shampoo into my scalp, a familiar question echoed in my mind: What was I doing to deserve this kind of behaviour from James?

Was it something I said, or didn't say? Some way I was acting that triggered him? I started mentally sifting through the moments we'd shared, searching for signs I might've missed. A wrong tone. A lack of affection. Something.

My thoughts drifted to Josh, another relationship, another version of me. Maybe I was falling back into old patterns. Maybe I still didn't know how to express what I needed without shutting down. Maybe I was sending mixed signals and James was only reacting to that.

But the truth? I couldn't see it. Not clearly. Maybe someone else could. Maybe it was time to talk to someone, family, friends. But I hadn't opened up to any of them about this. I didn't even know where I'd begin. And besides, I already knew what they'd say: **"Come home".**

The thought landed like a weight in my chest. Maybe I needed to find a therapist nearby. Someone objective. Someone who wouldn't jump to rescue me or tell me what I already feared.

Or maybe I was overthinking all of it. Maybe I was expecting too much, setting the bar too high, wanting more than he could give. Was that unfair of me? Still, I couldn't shake the feeling. I hadn't come all this way, all this distance, just to land back in the same emotional place I'd fought so hard to leave.

Chapter 15

James was on his days off, which meant my nervous system went on high alert. Whenever he was home all day with me, I felt unsettled. His presence lingered, even when he wasn't in the room. He had a way of creeping up behind me or suddenly appearing when I thought I was alone. I kept telling myself I was still adjusting to living with someone else. But deep down, something felt off.

Tonight was drinks with James's co-workers, and I needed to get my head in the right space.

I had an outfit picked out that made me feel powerful—confident. Still, anxiety tugged at my stomach. I was nervous to go. But I needed to be there.

Maybe because I wanted them to see I was with James. That I belonged. That he'd chosen me. Ping! My phone buzzed from the other room. A new email. I walked over and grabbed it.

It was from one of the brands I'd been creating book content for. Strange, they rarely responded so quickly. I had just submitted my review. I tapped to open it.

Dear Samantha,

I hope this message finds you well. We've been genuinely moved by the depth and insight you bring to your reviews. Your recent work has not only resonated with our audience but has also raised the bar for the kind of quality and authenticity we strive to uphold.

We're reaching out with an exciting opportunity for collaboration. As we prepare for an upcoming campaign, we're working on a tight timeline and would love to tap into your expertise and creative voice to help us deliver content that truly connects.

To honour both the urgency and the value of your contribution, we're offering increased compensation for this project, including a salary that reflects your time, effort, and expertise. Your voice holds power, and we believe it can make a meaningful impact on this campaign.

If this sounds like something you'd be interested in, please let us know by 8 a.m. tomorrow. (like we said, tight timeline) Feel free to reach out with any questions; we'd be happy to discuss the project in more detail and make sure it aligns with your schedule and creative vision.

Looking forward to hearing from you soon.

I just stared at my phone, stunned. This was it, everything I'd been working toward.

Security. Growth. A real future. The kind of offer that could shift the ground beneath my feet in the best possible way. I couldn't wait to tell someone.

Heart racing, I hurried downstairs to tell James. He'd be happy, he had to be. He'd been in a pretty good mood lately, and this? This was good news. Job security, real benefits. Something we could build on.

I walked into the living room, still glowing, and found him glued to his video game controller. A racing game. Need for Speed, I think. "Hey," I said, practically vibrating with excitement, "I've got some amazing news!" He glanced at me, thumbs still working the buttons. "Oh yeah? What's up?"

I took a deep breath, letting the joy swell in my chest. "I got the offer. The one I've been hoping for. Better pay, long-term growth, actual stability. It's everything I've worked for." I waited for his face to light up. For him to jump up, wrap his arms around me, share in the joy. "That's good," he said after a beat. "Congrats."

His tone was flat. Unbothered. My smile faltered, just a little. I tried to push past it. Maybe he needed a second to process. "It's not just good—it's huge. This could change everything. Less stress, more breathing room. We could finally start planning, really planning."

"Yeah," he said with a nod, eyes flicking back to the screen. "That's great." The rev of an engine from his game filled the silence between us, loud and jarring. I stood there too long, trying to hang onto the joy, trying not to feel the disappointment climbing into my chest like a slow leak.

"Okay… I'll let you get back to your game," I said, my voice quieter now. He nodded again, and didn't look up. And just like that, the moment was gone. I turned and walked away; the warmth I'd carried just minutes ago was already cooling beneath my skin. Each step upstairs felt heavier, slower. Like someone had let the air out of my tires. Deflated.

I walk over and settle next to Mischa, who's curled up on the couch. Gently, I run my hand over her soft fur. She lifts her head, meets my gaze, and then rests it on my lap before licking my hand.

"At least someone in this house wants me to be happy," I whisper. Shifting behind her, I lie down so we're side-by-side. Mischa stirs, stretching out and adjusting herself until she's curled into the nook of my legs like she belongs there. I position myself to get more comfortable and decide to close my eyes for a few minutes.

When I wake up, I assume I've only dozed off for a few minutes. I reach for my phone. 9:02 p.m. Shit. We should've left already. James is probably fuming. I jolt upright, startling Mischa. She lets out a long, luxurious stretch, sliding off the couch onto the floor.

"James?" I called out. "James, I'm so sorry, I must've fallen asleep. I'll be ready in ten minutes, I swear!" Silence.

I rush to the bathroom, snatching up my makeup bag. There's no time to do the full routine, so I settle for the five-minute face I learned on TikTok. Then I yank on the outfit I'd set aside earlier. One quick glance in the mirror. Good enough.

"James?" I call again, heading toward the hallway. Still nothing. I peer out the window. His truck is gone. I stare for a moment, blinking. Did he leave? Without me? Without even saying a word? I grab my phone. No texts. No missed calls. I call him. Straight to voicemail. Perfect. Just perfect.

I'm dressed. Ready. Might as well just go and meet him. The pub is loud and unfamiliar, the kind of place that smells like beer and memories you don't want to remember. I step through the double doors and scan the room, searching. I've never been here before, so everything feels strange, like walking into someone else's life. Then I see him. James.

He's standing at the bar, laughing, relaxed. And beside him is a girl with her arm slung around his. Lisa.

Lisa?

I stop in my tracks, frozen in the doorway. My chest tightens as though something invisible is pressing against me, making it hard to breathe. My legs refuse to move. The longer I stand there, the heavier the moment becomes, thick with betrayal, disbelief, something deeper I don't have a name for.

One shaky step back. Then another. And then I'm outside, stumbling into the night air. The cold slaps my face, sharp, unforgiving, but it doesn't dull the ache in my chest. It just sharpens it. I sit in my car, fingers clenched around the steering wheel, staring at the pub's glowing sign.

Should I go back in? The question lingers, heavy and sharp. But already, I feel the sting behind my eyes. The tears are coming, hot and unwelcome. I hate the idea of crying in front of him. Worse, in front of her.

A shaky breath slips from my lips. I try to collect myself, to steady the storm inside. But the more I try to reason it away, the faster it unravels. Anger. Hurt. Embarrassment. They churn together, indistinguishable now. A tangled mess of emotion I can't sort through.

Why am I the one out here, in the cold, feeling like the other woman in my own relationship? I glance back at the entrance one last time, foolishly hoping he'll come out. That he'll see me sitting here, come running, offer some explanation that makes this all okay.

But the door stays shut. And my phone stays silent. My jaw clenches. I threw the car into reverse, the decision made for me. I can't face him. Not tonight. As I drive back, a thought surfaces, quiet but persistent.

Maybe his ex didn't cheat on him. Maybe he did. Maybe it was a version he made up to make himself look better. Maybe she gave him everything, loved him the way he said he wanted, and it still wasn't enough. Maybe she didn't blindside him. Maybe he just didn't tell the whole story.

Back at the house, I strip off my makeup, trade my outfit for pajamas, and curl up in bed with Mischa beside me, her warm body pressed close, a small anchor in the chaos.

I open my laptop and respond to the email from earlier. The job offer. Yes. I accept with zero hesitation. Relief settles in my gut like a stone finally laid to rest. For once, I've secured something steady, something mine.

I check my phone, again. Still nothing from James. I sigh and set it aside, reaching for the book on my nightstand. If I can't be in a fairytale of my own, I'll lose myself in someone else's.

That's when I hear it. I must've fell asleep reading again. I hear Mischa growling. It's low. Unusual. For a Husky, she's quiet more often than not. Unless she's really trying to say something.

"Sam," a hand shakes my arm gently. "Sam, wake up." It's James. "What time is it?" I mumble, groggy as I reach for my glasses on the nightstand.

"It's 1:30. I just got home. Sorry we missed each other tonight." His voice is casual. "I saw you were asleep earlier and figured you were too tired to come, so I didn't wake you."

Or maybe you just didn't want to deal with me while your side piece was hanging on your arm.

"Did you have a good time?" I ask, sitting up. He reeks of cheap beer, whiskey, sweat, and the faint trace of someone else's perfume. "Yeah, it was a blast. I spent way too much money." He laughs, light and careless.

"Who went?" I ask, knowing damn well who was there. He must not have seen me standing in the doorway. "The whole crew, plus some of the other shift, Lisa, Jordan, Kyle. You missed a good night. Lisa was really looking forward to meeting you."

Sure, she was. Probably thrilled I didn't show up, more time to play house with my boyfriend. "Too bad, huh." "Yeah, she looked hotttttt tonight," he drawls. "I've never seen her dressed up like that before."

I stand, needing to look him in the eye now. Needing to hear him say it. "James... did something happen between the two of you tonight?" "What? No. I mean, she was flirting with me all night, sure. Even invited me to go home with her. But it was all just jokes."

"Jokes?" My voice tightens. "And what did you do while she was flirting with you? How exactly did you respond when she asked you to go home with her?"

I don't tell him I was there. That I saw everything. That I watched the way he leaned in, smiling. How he let her touch his arm. How he didn't pull away. "It was harmless, Sam. Just flirting. Look, I didn't go home with her. I came home to you."

All I can think is "*wow…thank you so much for coming home to me. It feels so good to know that after my boyfriend has been flirting with another girl all night, he chose to still come home to his girlfriend. You deserve a fucking cookie James."* I keep those thoughts inside though.

"So, she knows you and I are together, but still thinks it's okay to flirt with you and invite you back to her place?"

"That's just who she is. She's nice. You'd probably like her. She actually said she hopes to meet you, and wants to be friends."

"Friends? Why would I want to be friends with someone who doesn't respect me—or our relationship?" I motion for Mischa to follow me and walk out of the room, heading to the kitchen for a glass of water. The air feels heavier here, quieter, like the tension came with us.

"Sam, it's nothing. No need to get all mad about it. If you hadn't fallen asleep and bailed on tonight, none of this would've happened." He trails behind me, casual. Too casual. I grip the edge of the counter, my knuckles whitening.

If you hadn't fallen asleep and skipped out… So, it's my fault. That's what he's saying.

I feel drained—physically, emotionally, mentally. The past few months have been a blur of confusion, self-doubt, trying to be better, to be enough. And now, after everything, he's turning this on me?

A bitter laugh escapes before I can stop it—hollow and humourless. "Right," I whisper, my voice foreign and shaky. "Of course. It's my fault."

James sighs, rubbing his face like I'm the problem. "Come on, Sam. Don't be like that."

I turned to him, vision blurred with tears. "Don't be like what, James? Upset? Hurt? You think I should just smile and laugh because my boyfriend spent the night flirting with another woman, then came home to tell me how hot she looked?"

He shifts, clearly uncomfortable. Like this whole thing is an inconvenience. "You're making a big deal out of nothing." The words crack something inside me. Is it supposed to be this hard?

My chest tightens. Breathing becomes uneven. A lump rises in my throat. I try to hold it down, but the sob tears through me, sharp and unstoppable. Once it starts, it doesn't stop. The tears come fast and hard. My whole-body trembles as I break open, right there in the kitchen.

James's eyes widened. "Sam..." He steps forward, hands out, like he wants to fix something he doesn't even understand.

I flinch away. "No." My voice is barely a whisper, choked and raw. "You don't get to do this. You don't get to treat me like I'm overreacting when you know what you did."

I scrub at my face, furious with myself for crying—but the tears won't stop. James exhales sharply, rubbing the back of his neck.

"I'm sorry, okay?"

I breathe in sharpness. "Are you?" My voice is trembling, laced with something between heartbreak and clarity. He doesn't answer.

And that silence? It tells me everything I need to know. I turn away and press my palms into my eyes. I feel raw. Exposed. Like I'm coming apart. Maybe I am.

Maybe I'm finally realising that this relationship—the one I sacrificed everything for—was never going to become what I needed it to be. Maybe I've been lying to myself. Building a fantasy from the scraps he offered.

James steps closer, hesitates, then rests a hand gently on my back. "Come on, babe. Don't cry." But I am crying. And for once, I don't try to stop myself.

After a pause, his voice softens. "I'll make it up to you. I swear." In my head, I already know I don't believe him. I left everything behind for something I was so sure about.

To be his second choice… again.

Chapter 16

For the past few weeks, James has been leaving a vase full of roses on the kitchen counter, as if a bouquet could erase everything. They're beautiful, but I hate what they stand for.

One day, he slips an expensive watch onto my wrist, his smirk smug and self-assured. Like a price tag on an apology could somehow make it count. I loved the watch, but I hated what it represented.

Every night this week, he's been cooking dinner, lighting candles, pouring wine, playing the role of the perfect boyfriend.

And for a moment—just a moment—I almost let myself believe it. Almost. But just as quickly as it started, it stops. The patience fades. The temper returns. And we're right back where we were.

Back to me, questioning everything. Wondering what I did to deserve being treated like this. Was it karma, for how I left things with Josh? That thought haunted me.

I didn't scream or throw things or have some dramatic exit. But I disappeared emotionally long before I ever packed a bag. I shut him out quietly, inch by inch, until the space between us became a chasm. I stopped asking him how he was doing. Stopped reaching for him in bed. I let him talk and nodded like I cared, while already planning my escape in my head.

Maybe this was my payback. Maybe I came all this way to learn what it feels like to be unseen. To be the one reaching while the other pulls away. Maybe I needed to know what it felt like to be on the other side of detachment.

Maybe I had to learn the hard way—not just how not to treat someone—but how to finally stop letting someone treat *me* this way, too.

I need to love myself enough to walk away. To leave behind this carefully constructed illusion. To start over. Again.

I have to respect myself enough not to accept this behaviour from anyone, especially from someone who says they love me. This doesn't feel like love. And yet, here I am, spinning back into a spiral I'm not sure I can escape. At least... not yet. All I know is, this isn't the life I came here for.

Was this blast from the past meant to test me? Or teach me?

Maybe it was both.

Chapter 17

Dr. Grame sits across from me, legs crossed, her expression composed but kind. I blink. I haven't told James that I'm seeing a therapist. Frankly, I'm scared to. So I've been keeping these sessions to myself. Dr. Grame has been a safe space for me. She's been helping me understand and help me process through my feelings.

My mouth opens, but nothing comes out. "So… what you're saying is—this is a thing?" My voice cracks on the last word, barely more than a whisper. She nods.

"It's called the cycle of emotional abuse. It's a pattern, Samantha. Predictable. And… it's intentional."

She's waiting, giving me space to process.

I'd never heard it put like that before. I thought he was just an asshole. Well—I mean—he *is*. But there's an actual *name* for this behaviour. I thought maybe *I* was the problem. That, maybe I could fix it.

That if I just tried harder—loved him better, communicated differently—I wouldn't always feel like I was tiptoeing a tightrope. Or walking barefoot on glass.

"Here," Dr. Grame says gently. "Let me show you something. Tell me if it feels familiar."

She stands, moves to her computer, types something quickly, then steps toward the printer.

A moment later, she's back at my side. She hands me a freshly printed sheet of paper.

It's a simple diagram—four phrases, each one connected by arrows.

I read them slowly. My pulse roars in my ears.

Tension Builds.
Abusive Incident.
Honeymoon Phase.
Calm.

Step One: Tension Builds

"This is where the stress and conflict start to rise," Dr. Grame says, her voice steady. "Maybe it's subtle at first. Maybe you just feel his mood shifting, but you don't know why. So, you start adjusting. You try to keep him happy. You do what you can to avoid upsetting him."

I let out a short, breathy laugh. "Yeah. I know that feeling." My mind drifts. I think about how James would wake up some mornings and barely speak to me. No reason. No warning. Just… silence.

I always sensed the shift before he even opened his mouth, like the air in the room changed. He didn't need to say a word. I could read the tension in the way he moved, the way he avoided eye contact, the clipped sounds of his footsteps.

So, I'd start adjusting. Making sure dinner was on time. Keeping my voice light. Staying out of his way if he looked even the slightest bit irritated.

I remember this one time; it was so stupid. I texted him at work to ask if he'd fed Mischa before leaving that morning. I didn't check the message before sending it, it was early. The words came out jumbled:

Hi good morning, just wanted to know if you Mischa has eaten this morning?

It wasn't proper English, I admit that. But the meaning was obvious. A simple, "*What are you trying to say?*" would've been enough. Instead, he exploded.

He texted back: **I don't have time for your fucking stupidity.**

And: **You really need to learn how to spell correctly, or at least read it before sending it to me.**

He never did answer the question. I ended up feeding her just in case. And if she got two breakfasts that day, so be it. Why does he think that it's okay to talk to someone you 'love' like this? Maybe because he doesn't love me. I'm just another body filling the space in the house. Paying half the rent, half the bills. I'm a roommate that he wants to control.

It felt like I was always walking behind him with a broom, sweeping up the mess of his moods, trying to make things smooth before they cracked.

There were times I'd feel a wave of anxiety just walking through the grocery store afraid I'd pick the wrong brand of something he asked for. Eventually, I had to ask him for pictures of exactly what he wanted, or else it would end with him belittling me.

Before him, I didn't even know what anxiety really was. Not like this. Not the kind that arrives before anything actually happens. The kind that hijacks your body, leaves your chest tight, your thoughts racing. My entire system would lock up like a fire alarm blaring inside me but no fire in sight. Just the *fear* of it. Looming.

"So, what happens when the tension builds too much?" Dr. Grame asks gently. I already know the answer. I've known about it for a long time. "He explodes," I whisper.

She nods. "That explosion can be emotional, verbal, physical, even psychological. Maybe it's a screaming match. Maybe it's name-calling, making you feel small. Maybe he breaks things. Makes threats. Yells at the dog. Or..."—she pauses, her voice dipping into something softer "uses physical intimidation."

Blaming me. Me apologizing for making him mad. Silent treatment. Raised voice. Fists slamming into drywall. I press my palms into my thighs, trying to still the tremor in my hands. "Yeah," I say, almost breathless. "That part makes sense."

Dr. Grame studies me carefully. "What happens after?" I hesitate. "Well... he apologizes." She nods again and points to a diagram on her clipboard. "Stage three. The honeymoon phase." "What does that look like for you?" she asks.

I drop my gaze to my lap. My voice comes out softer this time. "It's like... he becomes the person I *want* him to be."

"That's right." She taps the paper gently. "But this isn't about love, Samantha. This is about control. The honeymoon phase is just another trap to keep you stuck. Because if it were bad *all* the time, leaving would be easier. But he gives you just enough hope to stay."

"Does he buy you flowers? Surprise you with gifts?" I nod slowly. "Yeah... he has. At first I thought it was sweet, but I actually hate it. It doesn't feel genuine or real." She exhales; her tone steady. "That's the hook. That's how the cycle continues."

"But why doesn't he just break up with me? Clearly, he isn't happy. Clearly, he wants other girls more than he wants me."

Dr. Grame's voice is calm but firm. "Because he won't be the one to leave you. He'll do everything he can to confirm the story he believes—that women always leave him. It's part of the cycle." *Geezus.* My chest tightens.

This is bigger than me. I'm not some exception. I'm not special. I'm just another chapter in his pattern. I built an entire love story in my head—based on nothing. A fiction I wrote, and he just acted in… until he had me.

"Samantha, are you okay to keep going, or would you like to take a break?" she asks gently. I swallow hard. "No, I'm... I'm good. Yes, let's keep going. I want to understand more." She nods. "Okay. So, what normally happens next?"

My eyes drop to the paper in front of me. The fourth stage is labeled *Calm.* "This is when things seem normal," she says. "Maybe he's still doing things to win your forgiveness. Maybe he's taking you out or being helpful. Things that feel like they used to be."

I nod slowly. "This is actually when I feel the most anxious. Like I'm constantly bracing for the next explosion. I'm walking on eggshells… waiting for him to start—" My voice cracks. "All over again." A breath shudders out of me, and then the tears come, hot and fast. I cover my face with my hands, but I can't stop them. *How did I let this happen?*

My mind is spinning, racing through memories I once romanticized. That stupid night we hooked up… I thought it meant something. I thought *he* meant something. But I didn't know him at all. Who the hell did I move in with?

Dr. Grame's voice cuts through my spiral, calm and steady. "Samantha, I know how heavy this feels right now. But please know—there are options."

"I left everything I knew for this life," I choke out. "What am I supposed to do now? I don't have any family here. No friends. No money."

"You may have left everything you knew for him," Dr. Grame says gently, "but this life here it's yours. You can decide that this part won't define your story." I pull another tissue from the box, dab beneath my eyes, and blow my nose. My chest still aches, but something in her words settles in me, like the faintest flicker of hope.

I know my parents would want me to come home. But going back? That would feel like… failure. Like admitting defeat. And I'm not ready to wear that yet.

"We're coming to the end of our session," she says, glancing at the clock. "I'd like to see you again in two weeks. Does that work for you?" "Yes." I nod. "I think that's a good idea."

I stand, gathering my bag and the folded paper in front of me. As I reach for the doorknob, her voice stops me. "Samantha?" I turn. She meets my eyes. "Trust yourself." A soft smile forms. I nod, just a little. "Okay." And then I walk out. By the time I reach my car, the tears are unstoppable.

I sit there, letting them fall. Letting it all wash over me the grief, the guilt, the confusion, the quiet wish for something better. Eventually, I wipe my face, take a few shaky breaths, and light a cigarette. The smoke curls upward. I inhale and immediately regret it. God, I need to quit this habit.

But it's hard. Everything feels hard right now. And this wasn't the time. Not yet. As I start the car, the road back winds past the resort again. I'm reminded of the time I thought about applying to be a server there just to meet people, to feel normal.

Without thinking, I turn into the parking lot. Something pulled me in. Maybe that's what she meant by "trust yourself." The pull. The gut feeling. The quiet instinct to follow something even if it doesn't make sense yet.

"Hi! Welcome!" The voice behind the desk greets me warmly the moment I step through the double doors.

Sunlight floods the open space, pouring in from floor-to-ceiling windows that frame a breathtaking view, the endless ocean melting into the distant lightly snow-capped mountains. I pause in front of the glass, momentarily stunned. "Wow," I say with a half-smile, "the view definitely doesn't suck."

The woman behind the desk chuckles. "Nope, not the worst view in the world, that's for sure. What brings you in today?" I shrug, still drawn to the scenery. "Honestly? I drive by here all the time. Today I just... decided to stop."

"Well, welcome," she says again, her voice kind. "If you'd like, you're welcome to wander down to the water and explore a bit. Or, if you're up for it, the restaurant next door is serving coffee and cookies. It's not fully open yet, but they'll take care of you."

"When does it open fully?" I ask, curious now.

"Our season officially kicks off in January. The resorts open now, but we're still ramping up limited amenities until then."

"Thanks. I think I'll take a walk, soak it in a bit. It's beautiful here."

"You're very welcome. And thank you for stopping by our little peaceful place."

Peaceful place. The words wrap around me like a warm blanket. They sound... right.

I glance one last time out the giant windows, smile to myself, then step back outside. The air is crisp and fresh, tinged with sea salt. I follow the path down toward the beach, taking in the row of cabins and tiny homes that dot the slope like a patchwork quilt leading to the shore.

Each one is unique, some compact and cozy, others larger, like boutique cottages. One even looks like a mini hotel. The stillness out here is disarming. No cars. No chatter. Just the soft hush of the wind, the distant crash of waves, and the occasional creak of a cabin's porch step.

I linger a moment, letting the quiet sink in, then turn toward the restaurant. The scent of brewed coffee drifts faintly on the breeze. It was so empty. So quiet. But what a beautiful place to eat, to enjoy, to just... *be.*

The swinging kitchen doors creaked open. "Hi! How are you doing? Welcome!" came a cheerful Australian sounding voice that felt warm and effortless. "Oh, hi," I said, startled but smiling. "I'm doing well, thank you. How about you?"

"I'm good! What brings you in today?"

"I'm not sure," I said honestly, glancing around the calm, rustic space. "I always drive by, but today something just told me to stop." I hesitated, then took a breath. "Actually... I was wondering, are you hiring?"

He stepped out from behind the doors, wiping his hands on a kitchen towel. "Yes, actually! We're still hiring for the upcoming season. We're looking for a few more servers and a sous chef. Are you here to drop off a résumé?"

"I wasn't really planning to. I don't have one with me, but I am interested. It's just... such a beautiful place."

"That's okay," he said with an easy grin. He pulled a small order pad from his apron and scribbled something down. "Why don't you email me? Just mention you stopped in and talked to me, my name's Eric."

"Thanks," I said, accepting the paper. "Can you tell me more about the server position?"

"Sure," he nodded. "We're looking for one full-time and one part-time. Part-time is about 20 hours a week, full-time is

35. Both get included in the tip pool, and the hourly wage is $18."

"That sounds fair," I said, surprised by how much I was considering it. "There's also the option to live on-site," he added, "in one of the staff cabins. Rent's taken off your pay at a reduced rate."

"Wait—*live* here? Like in those cabins by the water?"

"Yeah, those," Eric chuckled. "They're for staff. The earlier you arrive, the more choices you get. The prime ones go quickly once the season picks up."

"Wow," I said, already imagining what it might be like to wake up there. To start over. "Thank you. I really appreciate all of this."

"No problem at all. Hope to hear from you soon. Cheers!" He gave a quick nod before disappearing back into the kitchen.

"Cheers!" I glance out once more through the floor-to-ceiling windows. The view is impossibly beautiful, the ocean and mountains stretching into forever.

And for the first time in a long while, I feel something I hadn't expected to find here.

Safe. My hand hovers over the door. I hesitate. This is ridiculous, right? Just walking in here like my life isn't unraveling. Like I haven't been barely holding it together.

Like I can just hit reset with a job in a place that looks like a damn postcard. Can I? I've started over before. Survived worse. But do I have it in me to do it again? A quiet voice inside me whispers: If you don't send it, you'll always wonder.

That's what brought me here in the first place.

Later, back at James's house, I sit down at the kitchen table, laptop open. My fingers hover for a moment over the keys. Deep breath.

I find Eric's email address, attach my resume, and begin to type. The words come easier than I expect:

Hi Eric, it was great meeting you today. I am interested in a position. Attached, you'll find my resume.

I reread it once. Then again. I click Send. As the screen refreshes, a memory floats up Dr. Grame's voice, steady and clear: "Trust yourself."

Chapter 18

Between the self-help books, podcasts, therapy sessions, and a sincere effort to become more self-aware, I've started to feel a flicker of momentum—like maybe I do have the power to change things. Dr. Grame's sessions, especially, have helped me see more clearly. I can change my situation—but I can't change him. That's the part I've had to face.

And it's been the hardest part.

I didn't come all this way just to bend and break, trying to force someone that was never meant for me. Accepting that truth that maybe *this* wasn't meant for me—was gutting. I left behind everything I knew for a fresh start, but healing hasn't been linear. The road ahead? It's winding. Uneven. Sometimes it disappears altogether.

Still, there's one quote I keep returning to, like a breadcrumb leading me out of the fog. I heard it first in a book I'd ordered on a whim on a Facebook ad for **High Performance Habits by Brendon Burchard**, he offered a free copy, and since I was craving direction but short on funds, I took it as a sign. The Universe had nudged me, but the book sat unopened for months. Only recently did I crack it open.

There's a section that talks about courage and it struck something deep in me:

Ultimately, you must ask which your life is about: fear or freedom? One choice is the cage. The other - courage.

The realization shoots through me: I am choosing to stay in a cage even though the door is open. Even if the door was closed, I have the key.

Should love really be this hard? This painful?

Is it supposed to hurt in ways that hollow you out? To drain you, to make you question your worth, to wonder if you're even worthy of love at all?

"Relationships aren't all sunshine and rainbows, Sam" James would remind me. "Fighting is part of the relationship; we're going to argue about things. We're not always going to agree. There's no escaping it. So, you're just going to have to accept that this is how it is."

I couldn't accept it. All I could see was that damn cycle-of-abuse chart Dr. Grame showed me. It flashed in my mind like a warning sign. Suddenly, I was reliving every moment I'd questioned myself, every time I felt like I was the problem. Like I was too sensitive. Too reactive. Not enough.

It was like holding a mirror up to every single time I'd ignored my gut. I let out a shaky breath as pressure built behind my eyes. My head throbbed. A full-blown emotional hangover was coming on fast. Feels like I'd taken a hockey puck to the skull, one minute I'm okay, even enjoying life, and then the next, I'm blindsided.

Everything goes dark. Then I'm waking up dazed and numb, unsure what even happened. Everyone insists it did, but I can't piece it together. So, I act like it didn't.

But it did. It is. I'm not crazy. I'm not making it up. And I don't have to keep living inside it. Dr. Grame's words had sunk deep, echoing long after I'd left her office. "You can decide that this won't be part of your story."

God, I wanted that to be true. I wanted to believe I had the power to rewrite my life. But truthfully? I wasn't sure I did. How could I, when I felt like I had nothing.

Chapter 19

For Christmas, I bought James tickets to a concert out of town. Ever since I moved here, I knew he loved that band, he'd mentioned more than once how much he wanted to see them live. So, when I saw they were playing on the Mainland, I splurged. Tickets, hotel, even seats on the seaplane. I pictured us having a fun night out—something light, different. A reset.

But by the time the trip rolled around, I didn't want to go anymore. Frankly, he didn't deserve any of it.

Still, I told myself: This will be it. The trip that gives me the answers. I'd pay attention, really watch him—watch us. I'd come back with clarity. I mean, if we couldn't manage a single night out of town together without unraveling, what did that say about our relationship?

Our first Christmas together had been… fine. Mostly because we were never alone. We were always with his family or his friends. I'd actually found comfort in that. The buffer of other people. James was always on his best behaviour when we weren't alone. When everyone left, though, I felt myself bracing. Waiting for the tension to snap. New Year's came and went - it was like any other day with James—I was upstairs alone with Mischa and James was downstairs doing whatever he does, probably scrolling through Instagram, double-tapping on girls in bikinis. I was in bed by 9:30pm and James, actually he never came to bed at all. I found him the next morning sleeping in his tent outside. I never asked him why because honestly, I'm glad he didn't come to bed.

I knew it would be bad before we even got in the car. I wish I had listened to my gut—faked a headache, said I had food poisoning, anything. But instead, I did what I always did: I stayed quiet.

That morning, James was already irritable. Slamming cabinets. Huffing loud sighs anytime I asked a question. "Are you ready yet?" he snapped as I bent down to lace my shoes.

I swallowed the response rising in my throat. This is a test, I told myself. Just observe. See it through. One hour into the drive, I had my answer. Honestly, if I'm being truthful, I'd had my answer the first time he ever yelled at me, months ago.

James barely spoke the entire ride. I was driving while he scrolled through his phone, sighing at texts I wasn't allowed to see. When I tried to make conversation, his replies were short. Dismissive. Clipped.

And still, I stayed. I adjusted, like I always did. I let the silence take over. I told myself not to push. Still, I tried. "Where do you want to eat before the concert?"

He exhaled sharply, shaking his head. "Jesus, Samantha. Why do you always do this? Just pick something." I clenched my jaw. "I don't know what you feel like." "You should fucking know by now."

The words landed like a slap. I didn't react—just stared ahead, pressing my nails into the steering wheel. I reached over, nudging the volume knob on the stereo like it might drown out the sting.

How could I know? He's the one who needs every plan laid out—where we're going, when we're leaving, what we're doing—no room for surprise, for spontaneity. And yet here he was, pissed that I couldn't guess his craving. Another small fracture confirming what I already knew.

When the tension builds, you adjust. You try to keep him happy. You try not to upset him. Dr. Grame's voice echoed through my mind like a well-worn tape.

And I had. For so long. I'd bent myself backwards, sideways, invisible—anything to keep him content.
But for what? What about my happiness? Now, I feel nothing. No, that wasn't true. I feel disgusted.

Who was this man I slept beside? The one I moved across the country for? The one I let my sweet Mischa around? How had I gone from craving his attention to flinching when he walked into a room?

I'd ignored the red flags because I wanted so badly to believe in the version of him I first met. The one I imagined. But he didn't give me butterflies. He gave me anxiety.

Dinner was a fucking disaster.

James barely looked up from his phone. I picked at my food, silence pressing on my chest like a slow, steady weight. When the waitress came to check on us, she gave me a look—half sympathy, half rescue mission like 'Girl, leave this asshole. I'll sneak you out the back if you want.' I nearly smiled at her. And then, just as she refilled our drinks, he chuckled under his breath.

I should've let it go. But I didn't. "What's so funny?" He turned his phone toward me, smirking. "Just something Lisa said. She's such a flirt, it's ridiculous." Lisa. His coworker. The screen was still lit. A photo along with a text:

If only all the guys at work were as easy to talk to as you.

My stomach twisted. "Why is she sending you selfies?" James sighed, exasperated. "Oh my god, Samantha. It's not a big deal. Don't make this a thing." I wasn't making it a thing. He had shown me. On purpose. Like he wanted me to see it.

Like he wanted me to know I wasn't special. That there were others, just waiting in the wings. I set my fork down. My hands curled into fists under the table. Dr. Grame's voice came back again.

The honeymoon phase isn't love. It's control. If it were bad all the time, leaving would be easy. But he gives you just enough hope to stay.

I had been hanging on to that hope. But there wasn't any left.

The concert was fine—probably because we didn't have to talk. Except when I checked in on our dog sitter. "Justin took Mischa to the trail," I said in the car afterward. "She loved it." James looked over at me like I'd interrupted some life-altering epiphany. He didn't care. Not really.

I didn't sleep that night.

James passed out beside me, snoring loudly, as he does, except this time, I was more annoyed that he was even beside me while I stared at the ceiling. This can't be what I came all this way for.

I turned over, grabbing my phone off the nightstand. Opened my email to find one from Eric:

Hi Samantha, we'd love to have you on board! If you're available, come by this week to pick your cabin if you plan on staying onsite. No worries if you don't, we'd still like to have you. We're excited to have you as part of the team.

I stared at the email, rereading it three times.

This was real. For the first time in a long time, I slept through the night. In the morning, I woke to silence. No James beside me. No warmth, no weight in the bed. Just empty space. Am I dreaming? Where did he go?

The door clicked open. A keycard. Then footsteps. There he had two coffees in hand. "Hey," he said casually. "I was up early and saw a Starbucks across the street." He handed me one. I looked at the cup, my fingers pausing at the label. Did he even know how I take my coffee? My order changed with the seasons he never asked. Not once in winter. But... it was right.

Huh. Did he actually think things were okay?

That yesterday was good? "Thank you. That was... nice of you," I said, taking a long sip. Was this normalcy creeping back in or just another turn in the cycle?

James settled into a chair by the window, scrolling his phone like none of it mattered.

"I'll go get ready," I said, swinging my legs over the bed. "We can get on the road soon."

"Sure. Take your time."

Take my time? Since when has he ever let me take my time?

An hour later, we were on the road. He drove. Music played. My thoughts spun in quiet loops.

"You're quiet this morning," he said, lowering the volume. "Something on your mind?"

"Not really. Just tired. Thinking about Mischa... work stuff." I lied. I was thinking about how to tell him I couldn't do this anymore.

"I'm sure Mischa's fine. What work stuff?"

"I just miss her when I'm not with her. And there's the content planning, new books, the big brand campaign coming up." He scoffed, tapping the steering wheel with two fingers. "Right. Must be exhausting reading books and making videos."

I exhaled through my nose, trying not to snap. "It's more than that, James."

"Sure, it is..." Silence. I turned my face toward the window, watching trees smear past. I didn't want to be in this car. I didn't want to be with him.

"Did you have a good time last night?" I asked, testing the waters.

"It was fine. Until you started acting weird at dinner."

My jaw tightened. "Weird? Because I asked why your co-worker was sending flirty texts?"

James groaned and gripped the wheel. "God, Samantha. You twist everything. You're so damn insecure."

I let out a short, bitter laugh, the kind that bubbles up when you're just done.

"Insecure? Or maybe you're just an asshole, James." It came out sharp. A question in tone, but not in meaning.
His knuckles whitened. "Watch it."

"Or what? You'll go silent for the next two hours? Be my guest, James. I could use the quiet." That did it.

He slammed his palm against the dashboard. I flinched. The car lurched as he pressed harder on the gas. "Maybe if you weren't so suffocating," he snapped, "I wouldn't have to look for conversation elsewhere." His words hit hard, but I didn't flinch again. I wouldn't give him that.

I turned back to the window. Let the silence thicken. Let it wrap around me like armor. I light up a cigarette. I hate that I started again a few months ago but it's a distraction. James didn't speak again for the rest of the drive. And I didn't care. I felt nothing. I had given everything. Scraped the bottom of myself to find something, anything worth holding onto.

But there was nothing left. This wasn't the fairytale I'd hoped for. It was a slow-motion heartbreak. A nightmare I kept trying to wake up from. When we got back, James grabbed his bag from the trunk and walked inside without waiting for me.

He kicked off his shoes, dumped his jacket on the chair, and disappeared into his office, slamming the door behind him.

Three days passed like that. Three days of silence. No texts. No calls. No acknowledgment that I even existed in the same house as him. I wasn't sad about it. I wasn't anxious or desperate to fix things. I was relieved. Relieved because I had my answer.

Today was as good as any to sit here, out on the back porch, looking up at the mountains and getting quiet to listen to what I want. What I want is not what I have. The only thing that was keeping me strong all this time was believing that there had to be something better coming for me when I was ready to decide the time was right. I grab my notebook out of my bag and just started to write:

February 3, 2020

I am so happy to feel joy, love, and peace every day.

I have been consistent with putting in the work to reach this level, and it feels so rewarding every day.

My mind is at peace, my body is strong and beautiful, and my emotions are controlled and safe to express.

I am now financially free and have been able to live without worry.

All of my debts are paid, and I can live every day without that weight on me.

Professionally, I am showing up in a position that I truly enjoy and am passionate about.

My value is constantly being recognized, and I am earning an abundance in every area of my life. I am able to use my creative mind, be flexible with the use of my time, and my worth is recognized.

My love life is soaring, and I truly feel appreciated, valued as a partner, and wanted. He treats me with constant respect. He's constantly pursuing me and puts in the effort to show me love every day. I never question where I stand with him. His consistency and actions show me.

We make quality time for each other, we have fun, we enjoy each other and have an amazing connection.

He is the man I've been waiting for.

I feel lucky to wake up next to him and will always show my appreciation and love for him.

I now know what real love looks and feels like. Thank you for this life. I'm home.

As uncomfortable as it is to write that, to see it staring back at me, I know it's possible. But only if I choose to believe that staying where I am won't take me where I want to go.

During the silence, I made arrangements with Eric. I accepted a part-time position and claimed one of the cabins. I didn't care which one, just whichever was closest to the beach and allowed Mischa to stay with me. It wasn't a hard decision. Anywhere was better than here. I'll be there…soon.

By day seven of barely speaking, James was getting ready for work, and I was getting ready to leave and never come back. I had been quietly packing for days, filling my trunk piece by piece. I woke up before him. It had been almost a year of being here and I couldn't do it for another day.

I stood by the window, coffee warm in my hands, watching sunlight stretch through the trees. My heart beat steadily. Not with fear. Not with doubt. But with certainty. The kind of certainty a woman gains when she finally chooses herself—and the life she knows she deserves.

James shuffled into the kitchen, rubbing the sleep from his eyes. Still no words.

He grabbed his keys from the counter and walked out the door. I shook my head. All I ever wanted was for him to care. Not to treat me like I was disposable.

I wanted to feel wanted. Appreciated. Loved out loud. Was that really too much to ask?

He said he loved me, constantly, even. But how can someone claim to love you and still treat you like you don't matter? I had poured everything into us. But in the end, I couldn't make him happy. I wasn't who he wanted, and I wasn't willing to keep erasing myself to try to become her. I was expecting too much from the wrong person.

I spent too many nights lying in bed, asking why I wasn't enough. I questioned everything about myself, trying to justify his behaviour. Breaking myself into smaller and smaller pieces, hoping he'd finally love one of them. And then, in the stillness, I heard his voice in my head—echoes from fights past. Words he hurled when things got too honest, or when he was really arguing with himself: "You deserve better." "I guess I'll never be able to make you happy." It all clicked. He was right. I did deserve better.

He couldn't make me happy, not like this. Maybe the past version of me would have accepted this behaviour. That young girl on that cold New Years Eve night, but not this version. I'm not her anymore...

How had I let it go on for so long? He had shown me who he was—I was the one clinging to who I hoped he'd become. I had given him all the power. I was in love with a version of him I made up in my head, not the one who stood in front of me. I chose this. But I didn't have to keep choosing it.

Everything I ignored at the start? That's why it's ending now. As soon as his truck disappeared down the road, I grabbed the rest of my bags, put Mischa in the front seat, and drove away.

With every mile, I felt lighter, like I'd just shed a hundred pounds. Like I'd won the lottery. Like I was driving toward a new life. A new me. Mischa sat quietly in the passenger seat, her big brown eyes watching me. She knew.

I reached over and ran my hand through her soft fur. "We're going to be okay, girl." She leaned into me like she believed it too. Then she curled into her familiar donut shape and fell asleep. We'd be more than okay. We were on our way to a peaceful place.

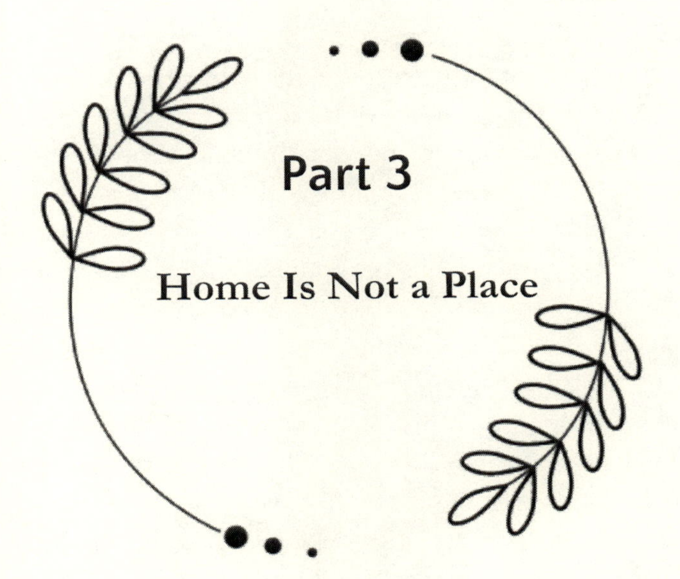

Part 3

Home Is Not a Place

Chapter 20

Hunter

Another good day in the books. I hopped out of my truck and opened the back door to let my favourite girl, Diamond, out. She comes with me everywhere, and has been by my side through every high and low over the last nine years.

We'd just returned from exploring the backroads near my place, our daily ritual lately. It's been my escape, my therapy, as I work through the wreckage of a recent breakup and piece together the life I know I want.

Inside, I went straight to her treat stash, dehydrated sweet potatoes, her favourite. She sat in front of me like clockwork, waiting. When I handed her one, she took it gently and trotted out onto the deck to enjoy it in the sun. Same routine, every day. She's predictable like that. Maybe she picked it up from me.

It was just past four when I headed for the shower, rinsing off the sweat and dirt from a day spent chasing waterfalls. Afterward, I pulled on a clean black t-shirt, a pair of jeans, then grabbed a beer from the fridge and the frosty mug I'd tucked into the freezer before leaving. Predictable, I thought again. But there was comfort in it.

Most days now, I am getting used to being alone. Really alone. In this house, in this life.

Creating a space for myself and Diamond that felt intentional—deliberate. Since Julia left a few months back, I'd committed to rebuilding from the inside out.

Looking back, I think I got so wrapped up in the idea of the relationship that I ignored the reality. I told myself it was a good match just because it functioned. She was kind. She had good intentions. She didn't do anything wrong. But we didn't fit. We were in different places, wanting different things. And, in the end, she saw that before I did.

So, when she left, I did what any self-respecting man should do. I faced the mirror. I studied my own reflection, ran a hand through my beard, and asked the kind of questions no one really wants to ask, let alone answer. *What's wrong with me? And what do I need to do to become someone the kind of woman I dream of would want to be with?* Since that conversation with myself, my days have been different. Filled with the things that make me feel alive. Intentional with who I want to spend my time with.

I took out some steak for dinner, for Diamond and me. These days, whatever I'm having, she's having. She loves being the only girl in my life.

She gets nearly every minute of my time. She sleeps on the other side of the bed like she belongs there. Every meal, she's right beside me. Honestly, if it weren't for her, I'm not sure how I would've survived the last few years. Through the heartbreak of my divorce, through the breakups that followed, Diamond stayed. Unbothered. Loyal. Soft eyes and a wagging tail.

I sink into the leather couch, its cool surface familiar beneath me. I let YouTube shuffle through an auto-generated playlist, background noise for the quiet. I reach for my journal on the coffee table.

For the last three months, almost religiously, I've been carving out this moment, just before dinner, just before the night begins to settle, for a simple ritual: Write down three things I'm grateful for.

Saturday Feb 15 2020

For the waterfall I saw today and being able to capture it in a beautiful way.

The way Diamond makes me feel so calm and at ease.

My job and the freedom it gives me.

I set the journal down, take another sip of my cold beer, and reach for my phone.

Earlier this month, I reactivated my Tinder account. For the first time in a long time, I felt ready, ready to meet someone new. Someone real. The kind of woman I've been searching for.

But this time, I wasn't winging it.

I'd written a list, a real one. What she looked like. Who she was at her core. How she made me feel. How our lives would intertwine with ease, not effort.

Taking that time, getting honest about who I wanted to attract, made it feel tangible. Like maybe love wasn't some fluke, but something I could call in.

I reach into the drawer beside me and pull out the letter I wrote a couple of weeks ago. The one about my dream girl.

Feb 3 2020

She has long, dark brunette hair. Big, expressive eyes that make me feel something I can't quite explain. A smile that lights up a room. She's naturally beautiful—the kind of woman who doesn't need makeup to feel good in her own skin. Curvy, feminine, soft. The kind of presence you feel before she even speaks.

But more than how she looks, it's about who she is. She's kind. Playful. A little sarcastic, but with a good heart. She believes in energy, in intuition, in things that can't always be explained. She knows how to be alone and doesn't need a relationship, but when she's in one, she's all in. She's open-hearted. Loyal. The kind of woman who makes you feel loved even when she's not in the room.

She's outdoorsy, but not in a performative way—she genuinely loves the forest, the sound of a river, the feeling of chasing a waterfall just for the sake of it. She likes breweries, trying new foods, curling up with a book that makes her think. She's comfortable in her own skin, comfortable with me.

This wasn't just a list I was writing. It was a manifestation. And I would recognize her when she finally appeared.

All this time, all the breakups, all the heartache and still, I believed she was out there. I spent so much time chasing the wrong women. Women I knew weren't good for me. But they gave me attention, and for a while, that felt like enough. It wasn't.

I made a promise to myself: moving forward, I won't repeat the same mistakes. I won't be the man I was before. I won't lose myself again. This past week, something shifted. I could feel it. Like I was finally moving forward.

I felt clearer. Calmer. Ready. Last Monday, I took myself shopping. A few new pieces: dress shirts, pants, a coat, shoes. Nothing extravagant, just something that made me look and feel good. I hadn't done that in years, if ever.

I wanted to look like the man I was becoming. A better version of myself. A man who walks with confidence. It felt like a turning point. Yesterday was Valentine's Day. I took myself out on a date to a brewery I'd never been to.

I sat alone, a little out of place, but surprisingly at peace. There was this strange familiarity in the air, like I wasn't truly alone. Like someone was waiting for me somewhere. Waiting for me to come home to her.

I open my phone and start clicking through my most recent Tinder matches, skimming their profiles again, wondering if I missed something the first time around. I didn't.

It all felt a bit forced like I was trying to manufacture a connection that wasn't there. I linger on the app a little longer. A few more women catch my eye, dark, long hair, soft features. That girl-next-door look. Sweet. Easy. But still… something's missing.

I close the app, stretch, and head outside to start the BBQ. Steak and Caesar salad are on the menu tonight. Diamond, of course, skips the salad, but I slip her a few croutons. I love the sound of her crunching, so serious about it, like she's working on something important. She's such a silly girl.

After we finish dinner, I tidy up the kitchen and grab her leash. Our evening walks have become sacred, non-negotiable over the past few months. We usually stroll all the way to the schoolyard, a solid 30 to 45 minutes round trip, before winding down for the night. There's a rhythm to it now. A shared ritual.

Back home, I pat the couch and invite her up. She rarely does, but tonight she climbs aboard without hesitation. Maybe she doesn't feel like being alone either. She flops onto the far end of the couch, her big brown paws stretching across the cushions, and lets out a heavy sigh like she's spent the day paying bills and managing a full household.

I smile and switch from music to one of my favourite YouTube channels, local photographers showcasing hidden gems around the Island. I love discovering the quiet spots that tourists haven't overrun. Diamond and I aren't built for crowds. These videos help me map out little day dates for us, small adventures that keep life feeling fresh, spontaneous, ours.

Suddenly, my phone chimes. That clean, crisp *ding*, the sound Tinder makes when you match with someone. It's kind of annoying, but there's something oddly hopeful in it, like a door creaking open. I reach for my phone, thumb it awake, and read the match.

Samantha, 31

Ready to meet the man I know is here for me.

I live on a lake in a small cabin with my dog, Mischa, in the middle of nowhere. I don't need you to be happy. I am already happy.

Clever and subtle.

I sifted through her photos and thought how gorgeous she was. Dark brown, maybe even black straight hair, which went down past her back. Big blue eyes, and a smile that would keep me in a choke-hold forever. Her frame seemed curvy and healthy. She had curves, which I am a sucker for and part of my non-negotiables. Her dog, Mischa, looked around Diamond's age, maybe a bit older, a Husky looking dog..

After looking through the photos, I send her a message:

Hi Samantha, well aren't you a breath of fresh air. You sound like a woman who knows what she wants, I like that.

I set my phone down and wait for her reply.

Chapter 21

Samantha

One week. That's how long I've been here. And still, nothing from James. No calls. No messages. Not even a half-hearted *"where are you?"* His silence is its own kind of reply. A brutal confirmation of what my gut has whispered for months: He doesn't care. Maybe he never did. I was just filling space until someone else—or maybe just newer, came along.

It's also been exactly one week since I had my last cigarette. I unpacked everything right away, as if rushing to start this new chapter. But I quickly realized… there's no need to rush anymore. I'm here. No one's waiting for me. No one's watching. No one to please or disappoint. There wasn't much to unpack anyway, a few books, some clothes, and Mischa. She wasted no time finding her spot on the couch, curling up like she'd always belonged there. She looked so at ease. Rested. Like she finally let go of something, too.

The cabin is tiny—maybe 300 square feet, but it has everything I need. Electricity. Running water. A small kitchen. Even a king-sized bed in the loft. I've never had a king-sized bed before. The first morning I woke up here, it felt like I'd slept for a week. No anxiety. No tightness in my jaw. Just… peace.

Making that first coffee with no one hovering behind me, no silent expectations, no tension in the air. That moment, just me and the mug in my hands, felt like everything. I could make this a home. My home.

From the balcony, the view is unreal, like someone painted the lake, the sky, the mountains just for me.

I catch myself staring, again and again, wondering how this could possibly be my life now. But it is. I pulled myself out of a place that wrecked my nervous system, that kept me in a constant state of tightrope tension. And I landed here.

Where the air feels cleaner. Where my lungs can finally expand without resistance. Where peace lives in the silence, not in spite of it. I decided my story deserved a better ending than the one I was settling for.

It hadn't been that long since I left James, but in truth, I'd emotionally checked out of the relationship four, maybe five, months before that.

It started the day he screamed at me because Mischa had peed and pooped on the floor again. She was trying to tell me something, and I needed to listen. From that moment on, I couldn't see him the same way. He no longer felt like my partner in life.

But it wasn't just that one moment. It was everything he'd yelled at me over the past year: shards of gaslighting, control, manipulation, insults, and casual cruelty that had piled up until I felt completely diminished.

I used to go to the gym religiously, skipped dessert, tried new diets not for me, but to avoid the sting of his comments. "Your butt's getting bigger," he'd say. "I usually only date really skinny girls."

Eventually, something shifted. I stopped doing those things for him and started doing them for me. That was the turning point. I realized I didn't need to change to keep him; I needed to change to reclaim myself. To become the woman I wanted to be.

The silver lining? All those expensive gifts he gave me designer bags, shoes, jewelry they held value. Just not to me anymore. I sold everything. It didn't even take a day for those reminders of him to be gone from my life. And I've made a promise to myself: I will never again accept that kind of behaviour from anyone.

I look back now and see how far I've come. I know where I'm headed. I'm no longer making space for people, places, or things that don't serve my growth. It hasn't been easy. Letting go of the fantasy I came here chasing felt like losing a part of myself. But accepting the truth was the closure I needed to move forward.

My parents have been calling and messaging every day, pleading with me to come home. And I get it they're worried. But I don't want to go back. That place isn't home anymore. I want to build something new here. I feel like I belong *here.*

From the moment I arrived, I felt a pull, an unexplainable calm that settled deep within me. Like something inside me recognized this place and whispered, stay. And even though it's only been a short time, I already see the signs: The bags under my eyes have faded. The eczema around my eyelids is gone. My gut issues? Vanished.

Changing my environment changed everything.

I didn't know how bad it was affecting my internal health until it wasn't.

That night, after cleaning up from my breakfast-for-dinner ritual, I curled up on the couch with Mischa nestled beside me. The air outside was crisp—the kind that makes you feel grateful for soft blankets and a warm room. I grabbed my phone, hovering between doom-scrolling and tossing it aside. And then, almost without thinking, I tapped open Tinder.

I downloaded the Tinder app earlier today. Not entirely sure why. Maybe curiosity. Maybe hope. Maybe it was the quiet nudge of believing, deep down, that something better might be out there for me.

The screen lit up: a few new matches and messages I hadn't noticed. I'd kept the notifications off on purpose, didn't want the distraction, didn't want to seem too available to an app. I tapped the messages tab. Three.

Brad: Hi Beautiful, I'd love to take you out one day. Where do you live?

Ugh. No. Delete.

Tyler: Hope you're enjoying your day so far. Just wanted to say hello since we matched earlier.

Yawn...... next.

Hunter: Hi Samantha. Well, aren't you a breath of fresh air. You sound like a woman who knows what she wants. I like that.

I sat up a little straighter. Huh. Different. Confident, but not pushy. I clicked on his profile.

Hunter, 45

Looking for someone to share slow mornings with, outdoor adventures with no set destination, and a love that feels like home.

His profile catches my eye again. I swipe through his photos, trying to remember why I matched with him in the first place. Four pictures each taken outdoors, either near water or along forested trails.

Always with his dog. She looks about Mischa's age, black with brown and white markings. Maybe part German Shepherd.

He has a full beard, steady eyes, and something calm in his expression. In every photo, he's wearing a ballcap and dark clothes, so it's hard to tell his build but there's something about him. Attractive. A little rugged. Mysterious in a way that draws me in.

I start typing: *Hi! Thanks for that. Yes, I do, we're only here once so I'm not interested in wasting the short time we have here. I just want happiness and peace. And from your profile, sounds like you do to and may already have that. I'm pretty happy here but it would be great to share that time with someone. How's it going?*

Within what seems like just a few seconds, he replies.

Hunter: You seem very self-aware, I like that. I'm doing great thanks, I went on an adventure today with my dog Diamond in the Nahmint Valley and now we're just relaxing on the couch, now talking to you. I live in Port Alberni, where are you? It says 130 km away from me in your profile.

Ohh, Port Alberni. I did a quick Google search to find out how far that is. Only two hours, not too bad. I'm reminded that I've travelled further for someone.

That sounds like a great way to spend an afternoon. What kind of dog is Diamond? She looks mixed? I live at the Summit Shores Resort. I'm a waitress here. Have you ever been?

Hunter: Diamond is a German Shepherd and Border Collie. She's 9. How old is Mischa? I'm guessing she is a Husky? Wow, Summit Shores. Looks like a beautiful place to live. I've never been, no.

Mischa's 13 and she's a purebred Husky. Well, I think anyway.

Hunter: She's got that Husky look. I bet she's a handful.

I glance over at Mischa and let out a little laugh.

"Mischa, he thinks you might be a handful and I think he's right, what do you think?" She just looks at me then turns her head the other way and rests it on the arm of the couch.

So, you've never been to Summit Shores? It's smaller than some of the other ones around the area, but it's so beautiful. Feels like a hidden gem. I've only been here a short time though but continue to explore around when I can.

Hunter: I just Googled it and it looks like something out of a magazine. How long have you been there?

I've been here at the resort for a week. I got hired for the season.

Hunter: Oh! Where were you before you got there?

Oh boy I thought. I didn't want to dive into it this early on but wanted to be honest.

I lived with my boyfriend, but we broke up, so I moved out and ended up here. Not a bad place to end up I tell ya!

Hunter: How long were you together?

I hesitate to reply in fear of him thinking that it's too fresh for him.

About a year.

Hunter: So Samantha, I'm going to ask what is it that you want? As in, what do you want in a partner and relationship?

Oh, he's just going for it, eh? I like that. No need to waste any more time if we're not the right fit.

I want to feel appreciated and wanted. I want the words to match the actions. I want consistency. I want effort. I want someone kind. I want every day to feel like the first day.

Hunter: That sounds wonderful. I believe in equal efforts for both. It's not healthy when one person puts in all the effort and is not appreciated. Do you have kids?

It sounds like he has been hurt before too.

No, no kids. You? I realize he is 12 years older than me and may have one or more. And that would be okay, depending on the circumstances.

Hunter: Yes, I have a son. But he's older and lives a few hours away. I'm a hopeless romantic and I'm searching for a special love. Like out of the movies or those country love songs you hear about.

I smile at the screen. I can understand what he means by that special kind of love, although I have never experienced it. Or maybe I never allowed myself to.

I get that. I also believe it exists. It's what brought me to the mountains in the first place.

Hunter: I've had small moments like it throughout my life, but not like what I know what I want now.

Okay, now I'm curious and I'm going for it. I realize he'll likely ask me the same question after.

Why did your last relationship end?

Hunter: I've been single for 6 months now. My last gf ended it. While we were good for each other in many ways, we didn't connect on a level that was serving either of us. So, instead of just accepting it as it was, she realized that she needed to take time to be alone, work on herself and heal through some things she hadn't been dealing with. Of course, at the time I was heartbroken, but I see now that it was a good decision. We are both better for it. We ended on good terms and I wish her well through her own journey. How about you? Why did your last relationship end?

Okay, how I could sum it all up.

Thank you for sharing that. Mine ended because the life and love I came here for didn't match the reality of it. While I could sit here and blame him for that and for the way he treated me, it was me who wanted him to be someone that he wouldn't ever be. It was me who needed to change. I wasn't meant to be there. But I do believe I am meant to be here..

I pressed send and read it outloud. **"It was me who wanted him to be someone that he wouldn't ever be."** The truth of it was heavy, James never lied about who he was. He showed me, in so many ways, that he was incapable of loving me the way I needed. And yet, I stayed, believing that if I loved him enough, if I proved my worth, he would finally see me. Finally choose me.

But love isn't about proving anything. It's not about bending and shrinking and twisting yourself into something more acceptable, more tolerable, more convenient. I did all of that, and in the end, it didn't make him love me more—it only made me love myself less.

I wanted to blame him. I wanted to point to every lie, every betrayal, every time he made me feel small. But the deeper truth, the one I had spent months avoiding, was that I wasn't just heartbroken over losing him. I was grieving the version of him that never existed, grieving the life I thought I was going to live by moving here—the man I thought he could be, the love I thought we could have.

And that grief was mine to carry. Not his.

I exhaled, my finger hovering over the keyboard. Then, slowly, I added: *So, maybe I stayed a little longer than I should've but I think it was a lesson I needed to learn in order to be where I am today. To be who I am today.*

Hunter: And who is Samantha today?

A simple question, yet it held so much weight.

I let out a slow breath and I started to type: *Samantha today is still figuring that out.*

I paused, then backspaced. That wasn't entirely true. I had figured out some things—things I once thought I needed someone else to tell me.

I tried again. *Samantha today is someone who no longer waits to be chosen. Someone who chooses herself first. I've learned that love—real love—doesn't ask you to prove your worth, and I'm no longer interested in convincing someone to see me.*

I hesitated, debating whether I should leave it at that. But I wanted to be honest, and honesty meant acknowledging the uncertainty too. *I won't pretend I have it all figured out, but I do know that I'm stronger now. I trust myself more. And for the first time in a long time, I feel like I'm exactly where I'm supposed to be.*

And suddenly, I wasn't afraid of his response. It felt confirming to just write that out.

Hunter: That's a pretty powerful place to be. I appreciate your self-awareness and honesty. I admire that. Thank you for sharing that with me.

I smile at that response and before I could type anything he sends another message.

Hunter: So, what is your biggest insecurity?

Oh, wow. Shifting gears here. Hmmmm. Okay, you asked mister. *My lower body.*

Hunter: As in your hips, butt, legs?

Yeah, I've never been quite comfortable with how big my hips and legs are and I've just always had a big butt, no matter how much I work out. Plus. I do enjoy pizza, so it shows LOL.

Hunter: Sounds like you fit the description of my dream girl. I'm a butt guy; I love a naturally curvy girl. It's one of my deal breakers. I hope you don't ever feel insecure about that, if you are ever around me.

I appreciate your honesty about what you like. What else is on that list of your dream woman? I write that, not expecting a serious answer but since he shared one of his non-negotiables, I believe there's more to that list.

Hunter: Well, I wrote a list of what I want in a woman. With precise details. I'm attracted to naturally beautiful girls, the girl-next-door look, who don't need to/or want to wear makeup to feel pretty. If she throws on a pair of jeans and a ball cap, I'm into it. Must have long dark hair, curvy, big butt etc. Do you want me to go on?

Lol, no I think I understand what you're saying. But I must admit, I don't wear hats, so I think it's best we part ways now...

I laugh to myself, hoping he won't take me seriously. But hoping he understands that I'm being honest, I don't wear hats.

Hunter: Lol. You don't have to wear hats but if you wanted to one day, say if we went fishing or something, I bet you could pull it off. What are your 'must-haves' in a man?

I'd love him to be taller than me. Takes care of himself, respect his body and mind. Doesn't have to be crazy athletic but does things to maintain his appearance and the way he feels about himself. I want him to care about his health and longevity. Kind eyes, I wanna know he's looking at me. Strong arms. A non-smoker, I just quit and I would like to keep it that way, so I can't date someone who smokes. Good, clean hands. I like facial hair.

Hunter: I like it. I don't smoke, never really did. Except when I was younger and would be out drinking. But it's probably been about 15 years since I had one. Also, I'm 6'3, so unless you're 6' 4, would that work for you? LOL.

LOL. I'm 5'6, so yes.

Hunter: Okay, next question - if money were no object, what would you do with your life?

I think about this for a few minutes before answering.

Honestly, I'd live in the bush, travel whenever I wanted to whereever I wanted and just be able to write. I've read so many books these past few years that I'd love to write one, or a few, of my own.

Hunter: What would you write about?

I'm not really sure. Maybe a love story. Maybe a story about hope or manifestation. Or all of the above. I've had some concepts over the past several years but haven't been able to get clarity around it.

Hunter: I'm in the very beginning stages of it, but I'm building a house a couple hours away, maybe one day that'll be the place where you bring your ideas to life.

My eyes widened. I had to read it again to register what he just said. Is he joking?

Are you joking?

Hunter: Not one bit. It's been a long-time planning but now it's at a stage where foundation will be laid soon and some trees are actually getting cleared.

I smile. Even though I don't know him and we just started to talk, the fact that he would even say that I'm included in his plans to make my dreams a reality warms my heart. Maybe it's bullshit. But maybe it's not.

That sounds lovely. So, what is your Zodiac sign?

Hunter: Aquarius, you?

I do a quick Google search to see the compatibility level and once I see it, I laugh. Why did I even look? Why does it even matter?

I'm a Taurus and looks like the internet says we're not a match.

Hunter: Well, Tinder confirmed we were, so, I'll take Tinder's word for it.

LOL.

I glance at the clock, 10:03pm. I should probably call it a night. I have my first shift and training tomorrow morning and I want to be rested.

Thank you for the wonderful chat tonight. I'm going to head to sleep now, I actually start my first shift tomorrow. But I'll catch up with you later in the day. Have a good rest of your night.

Hunter: Thank you, it was nice chatting with you too. Good luck on your first day. I look forward to hearing from you and hearing how it went. Good night.

I set my phone down and smile. I look over at Mischa and gesture at her to come outside for one last pee before we head to sleep, even though she was sleeping before I woke her up.

I kick off my shoes at the door and collapse onto the couch beside Mischa, reaching out to stroke her from head to tail.

"Hi, my baby. Hope you had a nice, quiet day here."

She turns her head toward me, leaning into my hand. Her eyes are calm, and her fur is impossibly soft. Maybe I'm imagining it, but since we moved here, she looks five years younger. Lighter somehow like something in both of us has started to settle. She's happier here, more at ease. And so am I. I haven't heard from James at all and his silence is all the closure I need to move forward. I guess I have him to thank for bringing me to such a beautiful place and for giving me this peaceful life I'd been wanting so badly. As disappointing and hurtful it all was, it definitely made me realize what I didn't want and what I wouldn't ever allow in my life. This version of me wouldn't ever allow someone to treat me that way again. Better things are on their way.

I grab Mischa's leash and open the door, waving her to follow me out. After a long walk, Mischa makes her way to her water bowl while I head for the fridge, grabbing a bottle of water and taking a long sip. She hops onto the couch and curls up, her spot already claimed.

I slide my phone from my pocket and pause, the memory of last night's conversation with Hunter still lingering. I hadn't expected to meet anyone interesting so soon—or at all, really. But there was something about him. The way he asked real questions. The way he actually listened.

It made me curious. Curious enough to wonder what it might feel like to really know him. But is it too soon to feel that way? Too soon to consider someone new?

I don't think there's a perfect timeline for moving on. It's not about being "ready." Sometimes it's about choosing, choosing to take a step forward, even if it's a small one. Even if it's just admitting you're open to feeling again. I start to type.

Hi! Hope your day is going well. My first day went pretty well - except for the coffee I spilled all over myself near the end of my shift and the basket of croissants I dropped on the floor. Mischa and I just got back from a long walk. I didn't ask you yesterday, but what do you do for work?

Only a few shorts minutes later, his name pops up.

Hunter: Oh no, not the croissants. That's tragic. Please tell me at least one was salvageable. You're right, we didn't talk about our jobs at all. I work as a consultant for several major outdoor stores across the country.

I laughed under my breath.

No, not one. I would have eaten them, but they had already surpassed the 5 second rule. Oh, that's interesting, how long have you been doing that, do you work from home mostly?

Hunter: At least you didn't drop any bagels though. Yes, mostly from home. It does require some travel here and there. I've been doing this for 4 years now. Before that I was exclusively in the stores wherever I was living at the time.

Oh wow, that's pretty cool. Isn't it great to find a job that can give such flexibility.

Hunter: Yes, it allows me the freedom and time to grow into a career, while still making time to do things that fill my cup, like exploring, fishing and hunting. Have you always worked in the Hospitality industry?

I laugh as I begin to type. *Oh, no. Like not at all. Lol. My main job is a book reviewer. I get to read books, create content around them and work with some big brands. This is my first time as a waitress, like ever. I've always been self-employed, doing freelance work. But when I moved here, I wanted something where I could meet other people and take me outside of where I was living. And without knowing, it has given me so much more than that, even in just a few short days.*

Hunter: You are a very interesting person. I feel like every time we talk, I get to peel back more layers. I'm wondering if you would want to meet for a walk with our dogs, of course?

I just stare at his question. Meeting. Right, that's what people do. I didn't expect it to happen this quickly. I don't know.

I glance over at Mischa and ask her, "are you ready for this? To meet someone new?" She doesn't lift her head; she's likely trying to nap after that long walk. I think to myself, it's only a walk and we need a walk anyway. What's the harm in that? I'll meet someone new, which was the whole point of coming here in the first place. I think about my work schedule and the only time when I would have a free full day off would be tomorrow, since it's a holiday.

Sure, that would be nice. Does tomorrow early afternoon work for you?

Hunter: It does, yes. We could meet halfway somewhere. Do you know where the Airpark in Courtenay is?

I don't, but I'm sure Google Maps can lead the way.

Yes, that would work fine.

Hunter: Okay, great. Let's say, 1pm? We can meet at the Kayaks.

Sounds good. I guess I'll see you tomorrow then! I lock my phone and lean back against the couch, staring up at the ceiling. A part of me wants to run, to cancel, to keep my world as quiet and controlled as it has been these last few days. But another part, the part that brought me here in the first place, tells me to go. To show up. To see what happens next.

Chapter 22

Hunter

The day started like any other. I wake up, let Diamond out, meditate for 10 minutes, make my tea, and read a few chapters from whatever book I'm into. Right now, it's ***No More Mr. Nice Guy by Dr. Robert A. Glover.*** I'm more than halfway through it, and it's been a revelation pulling back the curtain on the version of me I used to be, and showing me how to become someone else. Someone better.

I wasn't always this guy, the one who wakes up clear-headed, who sits with his thoughts instead of drowning them out with TV, beer, or someone new in his bed. A year ago, even six months ago, my mornings looked very different. Too many nights ended slumped on the couch, scrolling through old photos, re-reading texts, half-hoping for a message from someone who'd already made it clear: she wasn't coming back.

But I made a decision. No more waiting to be chosen. No more shrinking myself to fit into someone else's life.

I spent years being the 'nice guy'—the one who didn't ask for too much, who made himself small, who mistook self-sacrifice for love. Turns out, love doesn't reward self-abandonment. It keeps you stuck. So, I started choosing myself. I made peace with my past. And now? I feel good. Steady. Clear. Ready.

I set the book down and walk into the kitchen to feed Diamond. As usual, she sniffs her bowl and walks away. She's not much of a breakfast person these days. Lately, she has been waiting for dinner. Steak or chicken, usually whatever I'm having, I make extra for her.

"Feel like chicken tonight?" I ask. She tilts her head, ears perked, big brown eyes locked on mine. "I'll take that as a yes."

I settle into the breakfast nook, laptop open, the morning sun pouring through the window in soft amber streaks. A couple of hours of work before I drive into Courtenay to meet Samantha. Just thinking about her makes me smile. There's something about her. She's not like the others.

Even in just the few conversations we've had, she's come across as grounded, confident in herself, not rushing to fill a void with someone else. She doesn't need a relationship. She's open to one if it feels right, but she's not seeking it like oxygen. That kind of energy… It's rare. And magnetic.

I open my work program to catch up for the morning but just stare at the screen. My mind is too scattered to focus on anything remotely work-related. Fuck it. I close the laptop and start getting ready.

The drive in takes about an hour, and I don't rush. I'm aiming for that sweet spot neither too early nor too late. Since we're planning a walk and the weather's warm, I pull on my black spring jacket, a white T-shirt, and my favourite jeans. I hesitate at my shoe choice Blundstones. Not exactly ideal for a long walk, but they look the best with the outfit. If she's worth it, I'll suffer through a blister.

I pull up to the spot where we agreed to meet and glance at the clock: 12:53 p.m. Perfect. I grab Diamond's leash, open my truck door, and let her out. She gives herself a shake and trots ahead like she knows where we're going.

I'm nervous, of course but it's a quiet kind of nervous. Not the kind that spirals in your chest. Before, on dates, I'd obsess over everything. Would she like me? What would she think of me? But today, it's different. All I feel is a soft hum of anticipation.

I'm just excited to finally meet the face I've been talking to and thinking about for days now. I pull out my phone. 1:03 p.m. Then it starts to vibrate. Her name lights up the screen.

Incoming Audio Messenger Call from Samantha:

"Hello?"

Samantha: "Hey, so sorry I'm late. I'm here but I went to the wrong meeting place and can't seem to find where the Kayaks are."

"Oh, hey. Well, where are you now?"

Samantha: "In front of a Hotel."

"Okay, that's just up ahead from where I am. I'll head that way and meet you there."

I smile and feel relieved. I head in the direction of the Hotel.

The Hotel was not far at all. I started to see it and could vaguely see someone standing outside of where it is, facing toward the path I'm walking on.

It must be her.

Long dark hair that was half up and half down.

She wore a long beige coloured jacket that fell past her butt with black leggings that stopped mid-way on her calf, and pink sneakers. As I got closer, I got a better look at her face and I think my heart stopped for a moment.

She's beautiful. More beautiful than the photos of her.

In her hand she held a pink leash with a Husky on the end of it. Mischa. She's also more adorable in person. Her coat looks well-groomed and thick.

She walks toward me, eyes meeting mine. And for a second, I swear time slows down.

"Hey! So sorry about that. I'm not familiar with this area at all and just couldn't find the kayaks. So nice to meet you in person, thank you for making the drive here."

Grrrrrrrr.

"*Mischa!*"

Grrrrrrrrr.

Mischa growls at Diamond. Probably wondering who the hell we are and why we're in her space. I hear Huskies can be quite protective. I let them smell each other out. Hoping they will accept each other, at least for right now.

"No problem at all. Glad you made it. Nice to meet you, Samantha."

The Airpark wraps around a small riverside airport, nestled against the mountains. The views here are stunning, jagged peaks rising in the distance, soft ripples dancing across the water. The loop takes about twenty minutes, and if I had to guess, we did at least fifteen rounds before deciding to call it a night. My feet were aching, but I didn't want to stop.

In that quiet rhythm of walking, I learned so much about her, what brought her to the Island, the relationships that shaped her, the life she left behind. She spoke about her family back in Ontario her dreams, her fears, the way she's evolved over the years. It all flowed easily between us. No forced small talk. Just a genuine unfolding.

But when we said goodbye, she gave me what felt like an awkward hug and thanked me for the walk.

I couldn't tell if she was nervous and unsure how to say goodbye, or if she just hadn't had a good time. Either way, I decided I'd text her when I got home. Let her know I appreciated the afternoon. That I'd like to see her again.

About 30 minutes into the drive, a message came through the Bluetooth. Her voice piped through the speaker, clear and unexpected.

Message from Samantha:

"Hi Hunter, I just wanted to tell you that I had a great time meeting you today. I really enjoyed our walk and time together. I hope we can do it again sometime soon. Travel safe back home, and I'll chat with you later."

I gripped the steering wheel a little tighter, a grin tugging at my mouth. So, the awkward hug didn't ruin it. She actually had a good time. Maybe she was just nervous, maybe neither of us knew how to end something that felt so new, but already meaningful.

I wanted to kiss her. But I held back. It felt too soon. Too forward. Still... maybe she thought about kissing me too. I swallow hard, eyes fixed on the road ahead.

It's been a long time since I've let myself want something real. It's been a long time since I've believed someone might want me, not for what I can give, not for how easy I am to be with, but for who I actually am.

For the man I am now. For the man I'm still becoming. For the kind of man who draws in a woman like Samantha.

Chapter 23

Samantha

I'd be lying if I said I wasn't nervous, because of course I am. But it's the kind of nervousness that hums beneath the skin, the kind that signals something big is about to change... again.

I glance over at Mischa, who watches me from the bed, her ears twitching as if she already knows. Maybe she does. Dogs always know. And they don't just know, they tell you. Tonight, I'm staying at Hunter's for the first time. When he invited me, he was very specific: Mischa is absolutely welcome. He knows we're a package deal.

It's been five weeks since that afternoon at the Airpark, the moment something deep inside me shifted. Since then, we haven't gone a single day without talking. Morning check-ins, late-night conversations. It's been easy. Steady. I love the way he folds me into his days, like I belong there.

And it's not just talk, it's effort.

Hunter isn't a tall glass of whiskey or a walking red flag. He's a calm morning after the rain. A blanket on the couch during your favourite show. Safe. Warm.

I think back to our second date. The Waterfall.

I'd been there before, the first time with Mischa, and it had instantly become one of my favourite places. Enchanted.

When Hunter told me he'd never been, I knew I wanted him to feel it too. It was a five-hour round trip for him. Just to spend the afternoon with me. No complaints. No bargaining. No 'you owe me.' He was just... happy to come. Happy to see me.

I wasn't used to that kind of quiet consistency. That kind of love without conditions or scorecards. I'd dated guys who made me feel lucky to get a text back. Guys who would've driven five minutes tops and expected a gold medal for it.

So, when Hunter's truck pulled into my driveway after hours on the road, I didn't know what to do with it. With him.

It makes me shake my head now, how easily we accept the bare minimum. How quick we are to doubt the real thing when it finally shows up. That old saying "if he wanted to he would" rings in my head, a reminder that not all men are the same. Thank God they're not. I had so much unlearning to do. I'd spent too long expecting less.

I still remember standing in that parking lot, watching his truck pull in, heart pounding. It wasn't excitement laced with uncertainty. It was the calm thrill of knowing he'd show up. And he did.

At the falls, I don't remember the sound of the water as much as I remember the way he looked at me. "Worth the drive?" I teased. "Every second," he said. No hesitation, no question. And I believed him.

We headed to the next town over for a light lunch, and as we sat across from each other in that quiet restaurant, it felt like we were the only two people there. I barely noticed the other tables, the hum of conversation, or even the waitress. It was as though we existed in a world of our own, separated from everything and everyone, with only each other to fill the space. All we needed, it seemed, was each other. Our phones were tucked away just the two of us, uninterrupted. He was enough, and I was enough.

When lunch ended, we walked into the parking lot, and that's when it happened. Our first kiss. Unexpected, yes, but when he grabbed my hand and we strolled toward our cars, I could feel it in my bones. I needed to kiss him. Needed to know what it would feel like.

And it was everything I hoped for... and so much more. The third time we saw each other, he showed up again.
But this time, he came prepared. I had been working that morning, the exhaustion hanging over me like a thick fog. Half of me wondered if we should reschedule, but then a text pinged:

Hunter: On my way. Brought you something.

When he pulled up, he stepped out of his truck, holding a steaming coffee for me and a packed lunch. He even had a cooler filled with snacks and treats for the dogs. Setting up a little picnic beneath the truck's awning, he arranged two chairs facing the lake, the dogs sprawling out beside us.

And we just... sat there. Talking. For hours.

When he dropped me off at the resort, I invited him into my cabin. I wanted to show him how I lived proud and content in my little space. He stayed only a few minutes, but even in that short time, everything felt so comfortable, so natural.

Before he left, we kissed again, leaving me wanting more, but I didn't let it overwhelm me. I didn't want the physical side to overshadow the connection we were building. That's what he'd said, after all. He didn't want this to be about just that. He wanted to know me. Still, as he was about to drive away, I ran out to steal one more kiss. He probably didn't expect it, but I think he liked it. I shake my head, a smile tugging at my lips as I zip up my bag.

I've never known anything like this before. Someone who shows up. Who plans. Who follows through. There's no guessing, no games. No waiting around for the moment he changes his mind. With him, I don't feel like I'm walking on eggshells. My nervous system is calm. My heart? It feels… safe.

He wants this. He wants me. And the more I learn about him, the more I understand why. He's been married before. He's had relationships that didn't work out, some that left him questioning whether love was ever meant for him. But he never gave up. He kept looking, because he knew she was out there.

Instead of blaming others for his past, he turned inward.

He's doing the work. He faced his patterns, the parts of him that didn't align with the man he wanted to become. He's not just a guy looking to fill the emptiness in his life; he's a man who's ready to make space for the right person.

I exhale, my fingers brushing over the smooth surface of my suitcase, before I turn to Mischa. "You ready, Meesh?" I ask, scratching behind her ears. She stretches lazily, yawning dramatically, before hopping off the couch.

I grab her leash, my keys, and my overnight bag. My heart beats a little faster as I head toward the door. There's a small part of me that's holding on to this moment, reminding myself that tomorrow morning will be something special. A surprise for him. A waffle breakfast bar, elaborate and indulgent, complete with all the fixings.

This isn't just another night. It's the start of something I don't want to run from.

The drive takes two and a half hours, but the scenery is worth it. I've never ventured to this end of the Island before, and I can't help but wish I had sooner. Tall trees stretch to the sky, and everywhere I look, the mountains rise like sentinels, keeping watch over the lakes below. It feels like another world, one I could learn to love.

Mischa's asleep beside me, as usual. She's never been one for the journey. She's here for the destination. I punch in his address into the GPS. Only six minutes left. Six minutes from the moment that could change everything.

It crossed my mind a thousand times this date could go either way. But I've decided I'm ready to know. No matter what, I'll leave his house with answers, with clarity. And if it doesn't work out? I'll be okay. But what if it does? I shoot him a quick text: *Almost there*. I pull up to his house.

The gate wraps around the front yard, and the house itself is bigger than I expected. It's a bit much for just one person and a dog, but maybe that's how he likes it. I'm curious to see how he lives, what his space says about him. He's mentioned he likes a clean, tidy house. Let's see if he walks the talk.

I get out of the car, Mischa trotting alongside me. My suitcase and purse are a familiar weight in my hands. Before I can even knock, the door swings open.

Hunter.

For a moment, I forget how good he looks. His presence fills the doorway strong, assertive, yet strangely calm. So calm, it almost makes me uneasy.

"Hey, let me grab that for you." He reaches for my bag, setting it down just inside the door before unhooking Mischa's leash.

Mischa prances in like she's done this a hundred times before, disappears into another room, no doubt already making herself at home.

"Hi, thanks," I say, my voice soft with surprise. "Wow, I didn't realize how beautiful this part of the Island is. The drive in was breathtaking." I pause, realizing Mischa is already gone. "Also, I'm not sure where she went…"

"Yeah, I love it here. Don't worry about her, she can't go very far. Come on, let me show you around."

He gestures toward the living room, and we make our way through. He points out the bathroom, then leads me to his room, the room where I'll be sleeping tonight. And, apparently, where Mischa will be sleeping too. She's already claimed Diamond's dog bed as her own.

"Well, she wasted no time settling in," I say with a laugh, bending to pat the dog sprawled across the bed.

Hunter smiles. "I'm glad she feels at home here. Though Diamond might not be thrilled she's claimed her spot."

He sets my bag down on the hardwood floor of his bedroom. Its spacious two large closets flank the entrance to an ensuite bathroom. A king-sized bed, layered in soft blankets and plump pillows, anchors the room. It looks inviting.

He continues the impromptu tour, leading me into a bright, open kitchen. Everything is impossibly neat: the spice jars face forward in perfect alignment, the countertops gleam, spotless enough to catch my reflection. A pair of barstools perch beside the counter, and in the corner, a cozy circular table hugs a built-in bench seat.

I glance out the window above the sink. A wide deck stretches out toward the mountains, the sky bleeding into layers of early evening blue. The whole house radiates quiet warmth. It feels… like home.

Hunter nods toward the window. "Diamond usually camps out on the deck. She watches people, the occasional stray cat. Sometimes she stays out there until the stars come out."

"It looks like the perfect spot," I say softly.

He walks toward the fridge. "You want something to drink? Dinner will be ready in about an hour. I made roast chicken with salad and potatoes. That, okay?"

"Water would be great for now. And yes, that sounds delicious. Thank you."

He pulls a glass from the cabinet, fills it with filtered water, and gestures toward the couch. "I have something for you."

"Oh?"

He disappears into the bedroom and returns with a small paper bag and a folded piece of paper.

My fingers tighten around the glass. My heart kicks up a little.

He holds out the paper. "I wrote this for you. Wasn't sure when I'd give it to you, but... now feels right."

I take the letter, the paper warm from his hands, and begin to read.

...we both knew something was at work and it was only a matter of time before we met.

...I still don't know if I'm dreaming or a fairytale movie. If it is a dream though, I don't ever want to wake up.

...the moment your lips touched mine, I knew this was real and my life had just begun.

I deliver you this promise:

...I promise to never lie or cheat

...I promise to give my heart, love and share everything with you.

...I promise to not lose who I am in our relationship

...I promise to let you be the woman you want and need to be.

...I promise to protect you fully.

Tears start to fall from my eyes and roll down my cheeks.

...I promise to love you always and forever.

And as I reach the last words of the letter, I do something that I didn't expect or see coming.

I look him in the eyes and say the words. *"I love you."*

I can see his eyes are filled with tears too. He smiles at me with his eyes and says it with his mouth. *"I love you too."*

I lean in and we kiss. Except this kiss feels like love. Like we've just declared something permanent.

He hands me the small bag.

I pull out a small ring box. This can't be 'the ring' I think to myself.

I lift the top and inside is a ring. The ring is delicate. Silver. At the centre, a small yet meaningful detail of a diamond.

I look at him as if I'm asking him *'what does this mean?'*

"It's not 'the ring'. But it's a ring. To symbolize the promises, I have set out to you in the letter. To tell you and ask you to officially be my girlfriend in hopes that one day, maybe be more than that. But I intend to treat you as if we are partners in life."

A promise ring. I had never had a promise ring before.

Everything just feels so surreal. Six weeks ago, I didn't know this man even existed and now, we're together and it feels like we were never apart. I slip it on my ring finger on my right hand. Fits perfectly.

"How did you know my ring size?"

"I didn't. The sales woman told me that 6.5 was the average ring size she sells so I took a shot."

I just stare at it. Then stare at him. I reach for his face to kiss him again. I suddenly feel this rush to my heart. This was one of those moments where it feels too good to be true. But maybe that's what real deep love is. One where it feels so untrue because I've never felt this way before. Hunter wasn't just half-ass showing up or half-ass loving me, he was all in.

This isn't just a promise; it's a beginning.

Chapter 24

Hunter

The whole world feels like it's falling apart. Everything feels uncertain. I don't know what to believe or what to do. But one thing I do know is that I've fallen in love. Maybe it's the chaos of the global pandemic around us that makes this love feel so extraordinary. Like we've built something solid in a time when everything else is crumbling. Or maybe this was always meant to happen pandemic or not.

Every choice I made before meeting Samantha, every detour, every heartbreak led me to her. By all logic, it should have felt rushed. Reckless. Like we were sprinting through something fragile, skipping steps we were supposed to take. But it never felt that way. Not with her.

Every choice felt like the only choice. Like we weren't stepping into the unknown, we were coming home. Maybe time, for once, was working with us, not against us. Maybe everything had to break so we could see what was possible when you choose love even when the world tells you to choose fear.

It's been a few weeks since I gave Samantha the letter and the promise ring.

Since then, everything has shifted. Our worlds merged just as the world around us began to change in ways we still can't fully understand.

Samantha got laid off from the resort when everything shut down. That unexpected pause gave her time to visit more, to linger longer, to be here. And I didn't hesitate. I asked her to move in. Some people might say it was too soon. But I couldn't risk losing her.

I wanted to wake up beside her. To share my mornings and coffee and silence with her. To fill the big, echoing rooms of this house with her laughter. I wanted her to be part of the life I was building not as a guest, but as my partner.

Now, we're navigating this new reality together. A global pandemic has frozen the world. Businesses shuttered. Streets emptied. We're told to stay indoors, to limit who we touch, see, and breathe around. No one really knows what we're doing. We're all trying not to lose our minds. But in the middle of all this there's her. And somehow, despite everything, it feels like home.

We spend our days mostly together, but we've been aware of allowing ourselves to be alone too. We've committed the evenings to our date nights where we come up with themes and plan the date around that. One night it's a Mexican restaurant theme, tacos, margaritas and empanadas or we'd imagine we were going to a very fancy restaurant and put on our nicest outfits. It was definitely something we looked forward to. Since we couldn't actually go anywhere, we brought wherever we wanted to us and made the best of it. After dinner, we'd walk the dogs, then we'd all take a spot on the couch, watch a movie and cuddle up.

"You're quiet tonight," I say, stretching my legs out on the couch beside her. "What's going on in that beautiful, overthinking brain of yours?"

She smirks, nudging her knee with my foot.

"Just… thinking about how much has changed. How fast it all happened. It's wild, you know? A few months ago, I was somewhere else, with someone else, convinced that was the life I was supposed to want. And now, here I am."

"Do you regret any of it?"

She shakes her, "No. Not even for a second. It's just crazy to think about how close I was to staying in a life that didn't fit."

"I get it. I think we were both meant to wake up when we did."

She turns to face me fully, pulling her knees up to her chest.

"Does any of this feel… overwhelming to you? Us moving in together so soon? The house?"

I let out a breath, running a hand through my beard. "I'd be lying if I said I hadn't thought about it. But not in a bad way. More like—I never expected to meet someone I felt this sure about. And now that I have, why would I fight it?"

"You really don't second-guess this?"

"No, because it's you."

I reach for her hand, threading my fingers through hers.

She looks at me and shares. "I think I'm still learning how to trust that this can be easy. That love doesn't have to be something I have to fight for."

"I understand that. We both didn't expect any of this but I think that's when love happens. When you don't expect it and when you aren't forcing it to be there."

I've loved before but this feels different. I don't have to prove anything to her. She wants to be here, for me, for who I am. I wrote that letter one night after realizing that I don't want to lose her. That I would do anything to keep her safe, to protect her and to be here to go through this life together. In a partnership, as a team. I have been in relationships that I knew were wrong for me but I stayed anyway, hoping it would change, but it never did. This time it was different.

This feels so right and I won't go one day without letting her know that and making her feel that from me.

The plans I made for our new house were already in motion before I met her but now that she's in my life, she's part of the plan.

"Did you think while you were scrolling through Tinder that you would find everything you were looking for?" She asks with a big smile.

"I knew she was out there somewhere. It was just a matter of time. But I'm glad you showed up when you did, otherwise how would I know what colours to pick for the kitchen." I laugh while rubbing my hand on her knee.

"You're right, if we didn't match, you could've ended up with someone who picked out really ugly cabinets."

"That would be the worst thing ever. Every time I needed a cup or a plate, it'd just be another reminder that my dream girl was still out there."

She comes in closer to me and lays her head on my chest. "Well, it's a good thing she is right here then." I comb my fingers through her hair and kiss the top of her head.

"It's going to feel really good once we're in the new house," I say after a moment. "A fresh start. A space that's just ours. No history, no ghosts from the past. Just us."

"Can you picture it?" I go on. "Summer evenings on the front deck, the dogs running around in the yard. Waking up together in a home that we built, instead of just making do with someone else's."

She exhales and nods. "I can picture it. A place that doesn't ask us to shrink or squeeze ourselves into it—it already fits us. For this life." I hold her a little tighter. That's exactly what this is.

I've lived in so many places before, but none of them ever felt like home. They were just temporary shelters where I laid my head, but never really settled. Never truly rested.

In the beginning, when we first met, I wondered was it too soon to start making plans? But I've learned that love doesn't follow a schedule. There's no rulebook, no perfect timeline. If we keep waiting, what exactly would we be waiting for? Approval? Certainty? Time?

Why put love on hold when we already have it? The night I left her cabin at the resort, after we visited Lupin Falls, I felt it. When she came back out and kissed me before I drove away, I knew. I couldn't imagine being without her after that.

From that moment on, I decided: I would spend my life doing everything I could to be with her. Every love comes with risk, there's always the chance it won't work. But how else do we get to experience this fullness of what we feel, if we don't risk it? I'm done waiting.

I want to live this love story. Ours. The one I always believed was out there, somewhere. It took me 45 years to find it, but I'm here now and I have it. And honestly? I would endure every heartbreak, every wrong turn, every version of myself I had to become if it all still led me here. To *her*.

Chapter 25

Samantha

I wake up these days feeling rested, feeling like I belong. The August sun burns gently through the windows, its heat warming the floor beneath my feet. The air is clean, crisp with salt from the nearby ocean, and everything around me feels new. Not just because the house is new, but because *I* feel new. This is a beginning. Not one marked by fireworks or grand declarations, but by quiet clarity.

Mornings unfold slowly now. They're peaceful, intentional. There's no rush to be anywhere, no pressure to perform or pretend. We're just *here*, together. And somehow, that's enough. Somehow, for the first time in a long time, life makes sense.

I used to think love was something you had to chase. That if you wanted it badly enough, if you proved yourself worthy, it would finally choose to stay. But standing here, in this small house filled with light and second chances, I understand now. Love was never something I had to run after. It was something I had to be ready to receive.

Real love doesn't make you anxious. It steadies you. It doesn't take from you. It adds. It doesn't make you feel small. It reminds you of your worth. And if any of those things are missing, then maybe it was never love to begin with.

Having Hunter nearby makes that truth impossible to ignore. Just his presence grounds me. He radiates a quiet strength, a calmness that wraps around me like a soft blanket on a cold day. The way he looks at me, really *sees* me, gives me a peace I didn't think was possible.

Our bedroom still feels a little empty. The house is small, but it's ours. And really, who needs a big house when all you want is to be close? I felt the love here from the start. It's as if the walls shifted to make space just for us. The cozy couch we picked out together, the layout we changed at the last minute to better fit who we are. Half of the couch goes unused because nearly every night, we sit pressed beside each other, touching. Always touching.

Even the dogs have found their places. Mischa stretches out by the front door like a loyal sentry, while Diamond curls up in the spare room, which will eventually become Hunter's office. I don't think I've ever seen Mischa so... content. Every day, she seems younger somehow, like this life is giving her back something she'd lost. More energy. More light. More joy.

Same, girl. Same.

It's not perfect. The walls are still bare, the backyard is mostly dust and dirt, and the pantry shelves are only half-installed. But that's what I love the most. We're building this together—not just a home, but a life. I feel like I've unpacked more than just my physical belongings, but also my emotional baggage. It feels safe to have it out in the open.

I glance at the clock. Five minutes until my Zoom session with Dr. Grame. It's been a while since our last check-in, but I made a promise to myself: keep doing the work. Love didn't erase the old wounds. It just made me more willing to heal them.

I walk over to the window in Hunter's soon-to-be office and spot Mischa lying against the side of the house, her favourite spot in the yard. I catch myself looking for her more and more these days, needing to know she's still close. Huskies are notorious escape artists, but so far, Mischa hasn't tested the boundaries. She has the same freedom she's always had, and yet she chooses to stay where I can see her. That settles something in me.

I grab my laptop and head into our bedroom, settling cross-legged on the floor. I click the Zoom link, and a moment later, Dr. Grame's familiar face appears on screen.

"Samantha," she greets me with a warm smile. "I was just thinking about you the other day. How have you been?"

I hesitate for a second before answering. "Honestly? Happy. And that still feels weird to say out loud."

Her expression softens. "Why is that weird for you?"

"Because for so long, I equated happiness with waiting for the other shoe to drop. Like I had to fight or force it to happen. I don't think I've ever been…happy. I've tried to be, pretended to be, thought I was… but now that I actually know what happiness feels like, I don't think I ever truly was. Real love feels less like butterflies and more like an inhale of clean air and finally exhaling."

She nods. "That's a beautiful way of describing love." I go on…"Every time something good happened before, I prepared for it to be taken away. I think I did that with love, too. Believed I had to fight for it. Make it be something that wasn't. Earn it."

"And now?" she prompts.

I glance around the room—the house we've made a home. The life we're creating. "Now… I don't feel like I have to prove anything. I don't feel like I have to fight for Hunter's love. It's just… there. Every day, in every little thing he does. In who he is. In who I want to be."

She tilts her head, "And who do you want to be?"

"Better than I was before. I often think back to my first marriage and how inexperienced I was in being in a real relationship. I didn't know who I was, I didn't know how to communicate my feelings properly and I didn't show up for him in the ways that a partner should have. And he didn't deserve that. I don't want to do that again. I want to be with Hunter through it all. The good, the bad and the messy parts in between."

Dr. Grame has this look on her face, like she's studying me. "That's beautiful Samantha. That's really great awareness. This is why people say being in relationships takes work. But they fail to add that the work is internal. The work begins with us." She puts her hand on her heart and continues, "if we focus on bettering ourselves then only then will we show up better for those around us. But it starts with you. Only you have the power to change. We cannot change others to be who we want them to be. That's not our job."

"And that's what I'm learning. It's too exhausting to try. Since meeting Hunter and seeing who he is now, is who I want. Not another version of him. Not the potential of who I want him to be. But him, right now. It makes me want to become better."

"Have you noticed any triggers that have come up in your relationship with Hunter that affect you or make you revert to an older version of you?"

"There have been moments where something he has said made me react in a not so appealing way. It wasn't his fault or his intent but I took it the wrong way because it sounded like something I had experienced before. I expected a fight but I was the only one with boxing gloves on."

She nods as if she expected this. "That is normal, given what you had gone through and it being so fresh. It's important that you recognize that and realize that Hunter and anyone else are not the same person. Just like you aren't the same person as you were with your ex-husband."

"Right, I hadn't thought about it that way."

She continues. "How has it been since moving in together?"

"Well, when I moved from the resort to his place, there was a lot of push back from close friends and family. They didn't understand how I could move in with someone I barely knew so quickly, especially in the state of the world it's been in. It was a bit hurtful to hear their comments and constantly have to feel like I have to defend or prove my choices."

"What sort of questions and comments were you hearing from them?"

"They warned me that it didn't seem like a great idea because I barely knew him. But I was never concerned about the length of time that I knew him, that wasn't going to prevent me from being with him. I had already moved across the country for someone I thought I knew, why couldn't I move two hours for someone who actually wanted to be with me?"

"So, tell me what does this version of you want next?" she asks.

The question lingers in the air, heavier than I expect. Because I have everything I once dreamed of—a home, a love that feels safe, a life that is finally mine. But there's something else, something I haven't let myself say out loud yet.

"If everything stayed like this forever, with him, here. That's enough for me. I want to grow together, take care of each other, protect our peace and not take it for granted. I want that."

Dr. Grame smiles. "Then let yourself have it."

After the call, I shut my laptop and just sit there, staring blankly. ***"let yourself have it"***. The words cling to me like I need to believe it and live it, otherwise I'll miss it. I've wanted this life for so long, for something real, peaceful, something I could hold and not feel like it would slip out from under me. I was in survival mode, just trying to cling to whatever was there, whatever gave me a temporary feeling of happiness. But it never stayed because I didn't believe I could have it. I never allowed myself to have it.

I get up and open the door and head into the kitchen where Hunter is cooking us dinner. I love when he cooks. You can tell that he enjoys doing it by the effort and pride he puts into the preparation. It's not just ingredients slopped together. He is creative, sources the best quality and takes time on the presentation. Tonight, we're having a ramen bowl, one of my favourites. Packed with so much flavor in every bite, not too heavy and leaves you so satisfied.

"Smells amazing," I say, inhaling the scent of miso and ginger. He glances over his shoulder, smiling.

"How was your session?" he asks, carefully slicing scallions.

I hesitate, then say, "Good. Heavy, but good."

He turns off the stove, wiping his hands on a towel before walking over to me. "Talk to me," he says, his voice soft.

I let out a breath. "I told her how I finally feel happy, and how weird that is. How I used to think love had to be fought for, that I had to earn it." I meet his eyes. "But with you, I don't feel like I have to fight. It's just… here."

He tucks a strand of hair behind my ear. "Because love shouldn't be a war," he murmurs. "It should be a place to come home to."

I swallow hard. "I think I spent so much of my life proving I was worthy of love, I forgot to ask myself if the love I was chasing was actually good for me."

His expression softens. "And now?"

"And now I know the difference." I take his hand, squeezing it. "You're the first person who's ever made me feel safe without me having to ask for it."

He lifts my hand to his lips, pressing a kiss to my knuckles. "That's because you are safe. Always."

We moved to the table where he clearly set with intention. He lights the candles, uses fancy placemats, pours my wine and serves me first. I don't think there's anything this man does that is half-assed or mediocre. And that's just the way he is. He makes it look effortless.

"I think I finally know what I want," I say, raising my glass to his.

Hunter raises a brow. "Oh yeah?" We clink our glasses and he winks at me.

I nod. "I want to take everything I've been through and turn it into something meaningful. Maybe write more, maybe start a business that helps people navigate the kind of transitions I've been through. I don't know what it looks like yet or if it'll be helpful but I know I don't want to live my life reacting to the past. I want to let go of the pain and turn it into purpose."

Hunter watches me, the corner of his mouth lifting. "That doesn't surprise me. From what I've learned about you; you've never been someone who just lets life happen to you. It sounds like when something doesn't feel right to you, you do something about it. You rebuild. You take wreckage and turn it into something better."

I laugh softly. "It hasn't always felt like that."

"That's because you can't see it if you're still in the mess." he says

I let that sink in. He's right. For the first time, I'm not in the mess. I'm not running from something. I'm running toward something. Toward myself. Toward this life. Toward him. And it feels like exactly where I'm supposed to be.

After dinner, we do the dishes together, standing side by side in comfortable silence. My mind drifts to the last few years—the heartbreaks, the breakdowns, the moments I thought I'd never get through. I used to blame everyone else for not being who I needed them to be, for the pain they left behind. But as I rinse the bowls and watch the suds swirl down the drain, something shifts inside me.

If I blamed them for the pain, maybe I also need to credit them for the growth it gave me because of those experiences. As painful as it was. Because without those breakups, the nights I nearly gave up, the mornings I woke up with nowhere to go, I wouldn't have found this version of myself. I wouldn't have landed here.

Here, in this quiet moment, experiencing this peace. This breakthrough.

Later, we take the dogs outside for our nightly walk around the yard. It's nothing extravagant, but it's become a small ritual I cherish. The day may have been busy, but this time is sacred. No phones. No distractions. Just the night air, a little stillness, and the rhythm of walking side by side.

Sometimes we talk. Other times, we just hold hands and walk in silence. Hunter walks with that German Shepherd energy—protective and focused. There's something in the way he watches over me, not possessive but present. His energy used to intimidate me. Now, it grounds me. He shows up as he is. No games. No fronts.

And I find myself loving him more each day for it.

When we come back inside, the house is already quiet. It's late, and I slip into the bathroom to remove my makeup and go through my evening skincare routine—something I never really prioritized before living at the resort. But with a bit more financial stability and the time to invest in myself, I've started adding small habits that make me feel good in my skin.

Nothing elaborate. Just a few products that feel like care: a reliable makeup remover, a gentle cleanser, a hydrating serum, and a soft moisturizer. Even the way I use makeup has changed. I used to wear it like a mask, never letting anyone see me without it—especially not someone I was dating.

Now, I wear it because I enjoy it, not because I feel like I have to. I don't need to impress anyone anymore. And when I do put it on, it's for me.

I pull on my pink silk pajamas and head into our bedroom. Hunter is already in bed with a book, the dogs curled up in their beds on the floor. I leave the light on for a moment longer, then slide under the duvet and settle beside him.

I close my eyes, feeling the softness of the sheets and the warmth of being beside someone who loves me without conditions. Right now, I'm not performing. I'm not proving anything. I'm just me. And it's enough.

"Thank you for another beautiful day." I say to him then kiss him on the cheek.

He sets his book down and lifts his arm around me. "Thank YOU for being here with me to share this beautiful day with." He kisses me on the top of my head.

I motion to get up and turn off the light but he extends his hand out and says, "It's okay, I'll get it."

I lay back and shift beneath the sheets, getting comfortable. He walks over to the light switch by the door and flicks it off. That's when I notice them:

Several glow-in-the-dark stars are scattered across the ceiling.It takes me a moment to read what they spell out.

Then, the words emerge clearly:

WILL YOU MARRY ME?

I glance back and there he is, holding a ring box. The lid lifts slowly, revealing a soft light inside, casting a glow over the ring. I turn to him.

"Oh my God…" I squeal, loud enough to startle Mischa and Diamond. But neither of them moves. Mischa probably recognized it wasn't a fear scream, but a joyful one. She always knows the difference.

Still holding the box, he takes my hand and says the most beautiful words I've ever heard.

"Sam, I don't want to go through this life without you. You make me want to be a better man every single day. I want each day to feel like the first. I don't know what the future holds, but I do know I want to spend it with you. I want to protect you, provide for you, and spend my life showing you just how deeply I love you. I'm asking you to join me on this wild journey of life—growing together, day-by-day, as my wife."

I leap into his lap, cupping his face in my hands, and kiss him hard. Then I pull back, breathless and trembling, tears sliding down my cheeks. "Yes," I whisper. Then louder, trembling with joy, "Oh my God, yes. Hunter... yes, I'll marry you."

I wrap my arms tightly around him, burying my face in the crook of his neck. We just sit there, holding each other, letting the moment settle into our bones. "Let's see if this fits your finger," he says softly. He lifts the ring from the glowing box, takes my left hand, and gently slides it onto my ring finger. I study it, wide-eyed.

It's enormous. No other word fits. Diamonds everywhere. An oval-cut centre stone, framed by smaller diamonds along the band. "Perfect fit" he says. He's right. It's like it was made just for me. "Is this really my life?" I ask, almost in disbelief. "It is... if you allow it to be," he says with a quiet certainty.

I want to hold on to this moment forever. Wrapped in his arms, I feel safe—grounded in the knowledge that we both want this life, no matter how it looks or what lies ahead. If I hadn't learned what I didn't want, I wouldn't be here. I wouldn't have found clarity about what I did want. That clarity came only after I was brave enough to ask for help, to look within, to examine myself and finally say no to what was never meant for me.

I've had to take responsibility for my part in the pain, for the ways I kept myself stuck in places that weren't aligned with who I was becoming. Each stop along my journey was a chance to look in the mirror and ask, *who do I want to be now?* It was never about changing others or bending my life into something it was never meant to be. It was about unbecoming everything I wasn't so that I could finally become *her*.

Becoming her meant breaking down and beginning again. It meant rising through the rubble, choosing myself even when it felt impossible, even when it hurt.

Especially then. For the longest time, I was searching for a place. A house. A city. Four walls that might finally feel like home.

But home was never about the address or the keys that fit the lock. Home is a feeling. It's not about where you are. It's about *how* you feel when you're there. It's about *who* you are when you're there. I look up at the glowing stars above me. I see the words. I see Hunter's calm, steady eyes. I feel his arms wrapped around me. And I realize every decision I made brought me here.

There were no right or wrong choices. Just steps on the path that led to this moment. And if I had to, I'd do it all over again every painful, beautiful, messy part of it just to end up right here. For the first time, I'm no longer searching. I'm not running toward anything. I'm not running away either. I want to stay here.

Because this? This feels exactly like where I'm meant to be. This feels like…home.

ACKNOWLEDGEMENTS

This book took almost a decade to bring to life and not because I was perfecting it the whole time. I started and stopped more times than I can count. I questioned myself constantly. I got tired, distracted, overwhelmed. I wondered *who's even going to care?* But the truth is, I care. And that's reason enough.

To my husband Kurt — thank you for being exactly who you are. This book would not exist if you weren't the man you are: supportive, patient, understanding, and always in my corner. You are the man I always dreamed of and didn't know I needed. Every decision I've made led me to you, and I'm grateful each day for it. Every day, I fall more in love with you.

To Mischa, my heart dog, my witness, my companion through the messiest chapters of my life. You never gave up on me. You carried me through the darkness and led me back to myself with your quiet, steady love. This book carries pieces of you on every page and you will be in my heart always. Thank you for keeping me safe. Thank you for leading us to Diamond and to Ruby.

To my Mom, Dad and sister Carly - thank you for loving me through every wild idea, pivot, and plot twist. I don't even know if you knew I was writing this book but your constant support and love gave me the safety to keep going.

To my in-laws, John & Jill - From the very beginning, you offered me a sense of belonging, warmth, and acceptance that I didn't even know I needed. Your kindness, your quiet support, and the way you made space for me in your world has meant more than words can say.

To Christi, who I met in a random Facebook group (proof that sometimes social media *does* change lives) thank you for believing in this story and in me. Thank you for showing up for me every two weeks to read chapter-by-chapter. Your coaching, support, accountability and "boss girl" energy were exactly what I needed to finally start and finish something I'd been carrying around for years. Thank you for the guidance to finally get this published.

To Dinah, the very first book coach I hired to guide me through this exhilarating, emotional process. At the end of all of our sessions years ago, I decided not to write the book - to focus elsewhere. I have thought about it every day since. This book wouldn't exist without having those very real, powerful sessions together in the beginning.

To Laura, who helped me with editing and formatting - thank you for bringing your expertise, care, and sharp eye to this project. You saw the heart of this story and helped shape it into something I'm proud of.

To my Beta readers: my Mom, my sister Carly, Erin, Mina, Mariana, my husband, Kari and Kristen, thank you for taking the time to provide your early thoughts, deep feedback and support. This book would not be what it is today without you. Thank you for welcoming the opportunity to help me bring this book to life.

To Aimée, Ashley, Erin, Jasmine, Jennie, Karen, Kayla, Kelly, Kim, Lori, Lynn, Marissa, and Pamela, each of you hold a special place in my heart. Thank you for being in my life and for reminding me that this work matters.

And to **you**, the readers—thank you, with my whole heart, for being here. For turning the pages. For meeting me in vulnerability. I hope this story reminds you that you're never too far gone to begin again, and that you are worthy of bigger and better things.

Every choice, either the ones I made or the ones that were made for me led me to the life I live today.

Thank you for being part of my journey.